Goddess of the Moon

Book Four of the Immortal Kindred Series

A.D. Brazeau

Goddess of the Moon
Book Four of the Immortal Kindred Series
Copyright © 2019 A.D. Brazeau
All rights reserved.

ISBN: (ebook) 978-1-949931-30-3
Print: 978-1-953335-53-1

Inkspell Publishing
207 Moonglow Circle #101
Murrells Inlet, SC 29576

Edited By Audrey Bobak
Cover art By Maria Spada

DEDICATION

As always—For Brian and Quinn

A.D. BRAZEAU

The moon herself grew dark, rising at sunset,
Covering her suffering in the night,
Because she saw her beautiful namesake,
Selene,
Breathless, descending to Hades,
With her she had had the beauty of her light in common,
And mingled her own darkness with her death.

Crinagoras of Mytilene

A.D. BRAZEAU

CHAPTER ONE

Transylvania was the last place I expected to find myself. The irony of arriving for an extended stay in a region renowned for vampire lore was not lost on me. Not only was I here, I was in Romania to help vanquish a threat, not suck the life out of the locals.

The night's stars and half-moon were obscured by thick clouds. Even so, I could make out the mountainside perfectly. The landscape was not as I'd thought. I wasn't sure what I expected to see here; decay and abandoned castles, or maybe crumbling turrets with bats circling above. Instead, I was surrounded by a lush green, reminiscent of the land I left a few weeks before. The only eerie sight was a low mist that hugged the mountains like floating wisps of cotton.

The small cottage I would be renting looked rough, though. At least on the outside. This place would need some work were I planning on staying. Luckily, I didn't intend on remaining long. This was a job that should see me in and out of the country in a matter of days, maybe less. The situation didn't sound too bad. I had defeated worse in less time. This would be a vacation compared to Balor.

I stood next to the rusted-out, 1950s taxicab, once a

deep yellow, now a faded beige, and appraised my temporary home. The worn wood of the three-room A-frame building had once been crabapple red. Like the taxi, the vibrant color was now a distant memory. Its style reminded me of a cross between a schoolhouse and a Swiss chalet. The surrounding land was rocky and forested. Meaning, I would find myself deliciously alone.

The driver of the cab was attempting to pull down my trunks from the roof of his car with an audible grunt meant to draw my attention.

"Let me help with that." I tried not to make it look too easy as I helped the sweaty and limp-haired man set the heavy trunks on the wet grass.

He eyed me through narrow slits, no doubt wondering what lurked inside my heavy cases. Perhaps he was curious about what an outsider who looked like me was doing in this small city. My mother was an Egyptian queen and my father a fair-skinned Roman; the result was offspring who tended to take after one or the other. I mostly took after my mother and saw her every time I looked in a mirror.

My hair, curly and thick, was cut short, close to my head. In my life, I was forced to keep my hair long. Although feminine in my dress, I always envied men their short hairstyles. So, when immorality came, I whacked it off and have never looked back.

The man continued to struggle. It was probably best not to tell him one trunk contained as many of my ancient texts as I could cram inside, while tucked around my clothes in the other were swords, daggers, and other demon-hunting weapons. The texts spoke of magical objects, curses, and frightening monsters. Not something this man would likely enjoy reading.

Once both trunks were lying on the damp weeds, I handed the man a wad of bills I hoped would make up for his trials. He snatched the cash, jammed it into his pants pocket, and left without offering to help me carry my burden inside. No bother, I was glad to be alone and certainly didn't need help from a mortal.

Alone was something I hadn't been since meeting Bria. Having been solitary for a long time, I wasn't sure how I would handle not only a partner, but roommate. Now, I hated that she wasn't here. Leaving Alexandre and Bria was no easy task. I wanted nothing more than to continue to get to know my brother, especially now that he was mortal. I knew how time worked. For the living, it flew by and Alexandre was now a living, breathing being. But I had work to do. I would give them their space to get to know each other, to grow more comfortable in their relationship.

Before I could pick up the first trunk, I heard it. The dull sound of cloven feet pawing at the soft grass. Not a tone a mortal could hear, but for me, the scraping was as clear as a bell. The sound barely preceded the smell. Demons typically had some sort of pungent, unpleasant odor. This guy was no different. He smelled of days' old refuse rotting in the sun.

I scrunched up my nose, releasing my tote which contained my laptop, letting it fall without grace to the earth. It was a good thing I paid extra for the durable case. If I was reading the situation correctly, the creature had me in its sights and would charge at any moment.

I knew what it was before I saw it, but this was not one of the creatures I had been hired to vanquish. The martolea were deceptive shapeshifters who could change their form at will. This one chose the form of a medium-size hound, as they most often did. Their diminutive size would lead one to believe they couldn't possibly be much of a threat. But, as with a vicious dog, these guys were deadly and strong.

He didn't give me any more time for assessment. I turned toward the beast as he launched at my upper body. He was a little faster than I was. My knife, hidden from view, was underneath my shirt. I moved to pull the dagger from the holster secured to the small of my back a fraction of a second too late. Before I could whip the knife to the front of my body, the martolea barreled into my right shoulder, teeth flashing, saliva dripping from its stinking mouth.

"Ah!" I yelled as I lost a good-size chunk of flesh.

I spun toward my adversary and shoved him hard toward the ground. Off balance, he hit the soil with a yelp. Anyone watching might have thought this was animal cruelty. This was no sweet family dog; this snarling beast was straight from the literal pits of Hell.

Taking advantage of my superior position, I lunged, plunging the knife into its brain. The martolea disappeared in a puff of smoke. He would be re-appearing back where he belonged—in his Hell dimension. Nice of them to be so accommodating.

I stood, looking around to make sure I was alone. Hopefully, he was a lone demon and his pack wasn't nearby. Most lesser demons traveled in groups for greater strength. The night was still. A few crickets and a smattering of moths were my most sinister companions.

This attack was no surprise. Powerful beings sensed each other. The martolea, no doubt, sensed my approach and did what he does, attack. No wonder I was hired to come here. I pondered why these creatures had not been mentioned in the email. Perhaps my new boss didn't know what a threat they were. That must mean my other foes would be really bad news.

Not wanting to spend any more time out in the open, I lugged the trunks across the overgrown grass. The large boxes slid easily with a squeaking sound along the wet blades. My phone buzzed in my pocket, vibrating against my hip. I hurried inside, shoulder burning.

After setting the trunks on the knotty pine floor, I fumbled to get out my phone with one hand as I applied pressure to my shoulder with the other. The number came up as unknown. I was curious to know if this was the mysterious man who had contacted me over the web.

"Hello, this is Selene." I plopped myself down on the faded green couch. Surprisingly, not a speck of dust wafted into the air.

"Selene, wonderful. This is Joseph Whitby." The English accent was posh, every word articulated with perfection. "Are your lodgings comfortable?"

I looked around. The room was outfitted in only the necessities; the small couch I sat on and another opposite, a crate which served as a coffee table, and a yellow melamine two-person dining set from the seventies. The little kitchenette held a mini fridge, a sink, a coffeepot, and a hot plate. Lucky for me, I didn't eat food. I was sure the door adjacent to the kitchenette must lead to the bedroom and bathroom.

"It will do fine, thank you. Are we still meeting tomorrow evening?" I would let him know about my warm welcome then. No need to cause more distress. The shoulder would soon be healed, anyway.

"Tomorrow, at eight p.m. I'll text you the address."

"That will be fine. I'll see you then." I ended the call and moved off the couch to wrap up my torn flesh. Mr. Whitby didn't know I was a vampire. When he'd contacted me, I made an excuse about a sun allergy and said I preferred to meet and work at night. He hadn't seemed bothered, at all. In fact, he was glad, as demons preferred the dark for their extracurricular activities.

I shrugged off my ruined leather jacket and pulled my soft gray tunic over my head. That too was trashed. A clean dish towel found in a drawer would do as a bandage. This, I wound around my shoulder, tying it tight. I didn't have to worry about infection. My vampiric blood contained everything I needed to heal.

Most of my two thousand years on Earth were spent fighting demons and other nasty, paranormal creatures. Demons were not unusual, and it was a general term I used to refer to any unnatural being other than vampires and witches.

Demons roamed between this realm and their own. Often, they did no harm and kept to themselves. On occasion, they became more of a menace. There wasn't any rhyme or reason to this, just a traffic jam, so to speak. At other times, there was a more sinister explanation; usually, they wanted more power. This was the goal of the death god we sent back to Hell in Ireland. Hell was a general term I used to describe demon realms. There were many different such realms, all hellish in their own ways.

About one minute into unpacking, I realized I had barely packed any clothes. All the books and weapons I needed were here, but I neglected to think about what I would personally require, except for my Nikon Z6. My beloved camera went everywhere I did. I hoped I would find time to snap some shots of the countryside and local wildlife.

The rest was typical of my packing style. I would likely have to do a little shopping to supplement my wardrobe, especially since I lost my jacket and a top to the martolea.

I checked my shoulder. The bleeding had already stopped, so I wasn't in danger of ruining another blouse. I pulled a fresh white tunic over my head, then laid out the rest of my clothes. My style was casual comfort; soft leggings, flowing pants, and long tunics and sweaters. Alexandre called it resort wear. I called it comfortable.

A sense of loneliness hit me as I thought of my friend, Bria. It was nice to have a colleague, someone to plan with, fight with, and in general, hang out with.

Bria, a human, had become very dear to me in a short amount of time. Her personality demanded it.

There was any number of avenues I could have gone through to find an assistant for this job. However, trusting people wasn't easy for me. There had to be something special about them, or as in the case of Alexandre, a blood connection. Besides, I had no plans to share the prize awarded for a task well done.

I was eager to get started. This job should prove a lot easier than my last one. I say *job* loosely, as I don't get paid. Occasionally, I do receive payment in the form of a magical object or text from the local people I assist. This time, the magical object that would act as payment was the

Necromancy Wand. This wand had the power to raise the dead. I dearly wished to get my digits on it. In the wrong hands, the wand could be very ill-used. I wasn't sure if I would ever wield it for its intended purpose, but an object of such power could be manipulated for other uses, as well.

I was interested to find out how the man who hired me acquired the object. As far as I knew, the wand hadn't been seen in about four hundred years. The last known person to possess the wand was a Salem witch. When the witch was hung on the gallows, the wand clutched in her hand, it had simply disappeared. This was magic itself as magical objects are hard to destroy.

Mr. Whitby had contacted me via a group of people I worked with once in Brazil. There were a few local demons wreaking havoc in the Romanian mountainside and he wished them exterminated. Seemed easy enough, as these demons were all the lesser variety. There was no evil God of Death controlling them here and after all, vanquishing evil creatures was what I did.

To ease my loneliness, I called my brother. I left Wexford the night he became mortal. I had been contacted by Mr. Whitby that very day. It felt prudent to clear out and give the two love birds some space.

It was three more weeks before I heard from Whitby again. During that time, I went to France to peruse the shops for books I may find useful. We finalized our deal and I arrived from Paris.

Although Alexandre was now human, he was keeping rather late hours. Alexandre decided to retain the name he had used for the last two millennia rather than his given name of Caesarion. This was for practical reasons, as all his assets were tied to the former. Rather than go by two different names, we all thought it best to stick with Alexandre.

He answered on the first ring. "Selene, shouldn't you be chasing demons through Dracula's castle, covered in toxic blood and guts?"

I laughed, twisting Cleopatra's lapis scarab ring around my finger. "That's tomorrow night. How is everything there?"

Alexandre was silent for a beat, which made me a little nervous. "We're good. Bria's been terribly sick, though, and cursing my name to the skies. I swear, when that woman gets mad, her accent is so thick I can't understand a word she's saying."

"That's probably a good thing. How sick is she?" I felt uncomfortable thinking about an ill Bria.

Alexandre chuckled. "Nausea and the like. Pretty par for the course when you're expecting, but don't try and tell Bria that."

I gasped and jumped off the couch. "Expecting? It's only been a few weeks. How did this happen so quickly?"

"Slow down, sis. I'm sure you don't need a biology lesson. Let's just say that when you haven't had to think about birth control for 2,000 years, it's hard to get with the times. Apparently, our fiery redhead hasn't been feeling well for days but didn't want to tell me until she was completely sure. At first, she was thrilled—we both were. Now that the sickness has increased ten-fold, she's not so happy."

I tried to think back to my own pregnancies. They were so long ago, it was hard to remember, hard to go there without feeling pain in my heart. "I'm sure she isn't. Bria doesn't like what she can't control. Be understanding, Alexandre. She'll start to feel better soon."

I heard Alexandre scoff over the phone. "Of course, I'm understanding. I'm waiting on her hand and foot and dodging her knickknack-throwing with ease."

I tried not to laugh but burst out with a loud guffaw. A scenario of Bria lying ill in bed, throwing a lamp at Alexandre while he brought her crackers and water, was not difficult to imagine.

"All right, all right, sis. Go kill some demons and I'll check in with you in a couple of days."

"You're sure you don't need me? I can be there

tomorrow if you say the word." I had never left a job unfinished before, but my family came first.

"I doubt Bria would want you to leave. Besides, it may be more dangerous here than the mountains of Romania. Keep on fighting the fight and we'll see you soon."

Alexandre was right. Still, I longed to be back in the place I was surprised to consider home. "Kiss her for me."

Bria and Alexandre were talking about marrying. I wanted to ask if this would speed things up but figured it wasn't the time. If I was invited to the ceremony, they could do whatever they liked.

Alexandre may not have understood the importance of Bria's pregnancy with the same eyes I did. He was too busy dealing with the early days of his love being with child. A baby from Alexandre meant our mother's line would continue in the modern age. I had to sit back down to take this in. Cleopatra's divine line would live on. This child would mean so much and would be protected by her aunt at all costs.

A howl, distinct and plaintive, wailed outside. I jumped off the couch for the second time, the hairs on the back of my neck standing on end. Only one creature I knew could make a sound like that. There were werewolves in Brasov.

A.D. BRAZEAU

CHAPTER TWO

Werewolves were a dying species. I hadn't had many encounters with weres. The last was almost three centuries ago in Spain. I was attending a ball at the court of Charles III when a woman rushed into the main hall covered in blood. Her silk polonaise was in tatters, and severe lacerations on her arms and hands poured blood onto the marble floor. The woman was in shock, mumbling about a dog-man who had torn her lover to shreds before her eyes.

I'd edged to the side of the room, away from the spectacle. The best thing I could have done for the woman and the people in that room was find the beast responsible. Find him I did. He was a wild thing, feral and young.

The weres of Brasov sounded far enough away. My guess was they were deep in the mountains. Like Bigfoot, weres were elusive creatures. I felt I couldn't begin in earnest until after I met with Mr. Whitby. I also needed fuel for the fighting to come.

I was feeling peckish after my travels. My journey consisted of being cooped up in a train car with blacked-out windows. This was the more practical way to travel with my large trunks. Hiding myself on tops of trees and buildings was easy enough, but hiding myself and two giant pieces of luggage, not so much. An early-evening snack was exactly what I needed to quench my thirst before the meeting with Mr. Whitby. A small drink from an unsuspecting loner or two could do wonders, no killing necessary.

The evening was cool, pleasantly so, with a gentle breeze that smelled of grass and fresh leaves. I was right outside the city of Brasov, with the Southern Carpathian Mountains looming behind me. The range of jagged peaks was long, winding its way through Central and Eastern Europe. More creatures than demons lurked within its forests. I hoped the non-were wolves and bears were steering clear of the nefarious infestation. Animals had better instincts than humans and knew when to stay out of the way.

I didn't sense a single beast on my way to the town. This was a good thing for the townspeople. They must be keeping mostly to the mountainside. Demons and other otherworldly creatures were drawn to less-populated areas, stealing into towns and cities under the cover of night to grab a victim for their fiendish delights.

Brasov was a largely populated area, yet it felt more like a village to me than a city. This was mostly due to its charming, old-world feel. I loved cities like this and enjoyed taking in the medieval architecture. I imagined jumping from red rooftop to red rooftop would be a breeze, the close rows of buildings creating a pathway above the mortals below. As it was, I strolled down the cobblestone street, looking for an easy snack.

I spied a young woman, walking alone down the deserted, hazy, lamp-lit street. She seemed so vulnerable, so unprotected, and my heart went out to her. Although what I was about to do would cause her no lasting harm, I always felt it was an unfair assault. My brother would surely disagree.

The woman's jeans were modern, and her head and shoulders were draped in a gauzy white shawl. She wore a leather satchel across her body. The satchel appeared handmade by an artisan. The craftsmanship was evident by the top-quality leather and perfect stitching. I admired the camelia etched into the soft leather and painted white.

I crept up behind her, about to take her by the arm, when she spun around. I couldn't have been more shocked when she threw an arm up in a defensive posture and flung out her leg, landing a very solid kick to my mid-section. She was human, so the kick had no effect, other than to knock me back a little and surprise the hell out of me.

I placed a hand on my belly, rubbing the offended area. I affected the expression of an innocent bystander; eyes wide, mouth open. "What was that for?"

"You tell me." Her accent was lovely, her words as crisp as her pale-blue eyes. "You're the one skulking about in the night. I'm well within my rights to defend myself." She remained standing with her feet firmly planted and her left arm up to block me.

I smiled, nodding my head. "Good for you. And great kick. I was only going to ask for directions, but I love a fellow woman who can handle herself."

She relaxed, lowering her arm about halfway. "A tourist, I should have known. Where do you wish to go?"

"Somewhere I can grab a good cup of coffee." I lied, having no intention now of drinking from this awesome girl. I would have to find someone else.

"You're lucky. The best place is close. It's two blocks in that direction." She pointed to the west. "I can show you; I was going there myself to work. It's the only place open so late on a weekday."

"Wonderful." I stuck out my hand, "I'm Selene."

She lowered her left hand out of its position, grasping mine with her right. Her face hadn't warmed any, but at least her body was more relaxed. "Ileana. I apologize if I hurt you, Selene."

I patted my stomach. "Don't worry about me. I'm pretty tough."

We fell into step alongside each other, heading farther into the town. I felt as if I was walking into an old movie. I continued to marvel at the beautiful feeling the buildings and street evoked. I expected to see an old woman playing a violin; she never appeared. Everything felt a little close together, but not in a claustrophobic way. This was the kind of place I loved, nothing modern interested me too much.

Ileana watched me out of the corner of her eye as we walked along. She was frightened. Was it the beasts terrorizing the night that had her so scared and on guard?

"Are you from Brasov?" I ventured.

"I've lived here all my life," she replied. "Where are you visiting from? It must be somewhere far, like Canada or America."

"At the moment, my home base is in Ireland. I love it, but I very much enjoy traveling to new places." My accent could change based on where I was spending time. This was a conscious choice I made many years ago to blend in. When Alexandre came to Ireland, my accent began to mirror his and I hadn't done anything to change it. Currently, I sounded very American.

"Home base? What does that mean?" Suspicion crept into her voice. Ileana seemed very much like me, unsure of who to trust. I could appreciate her caution.

"Yes, my job moves me around quite a bit," I said quickly, hoping she wouldn't ask me right away what I did for a living. I better come up with something good. "Tell me about Transylvania. What do you love most about it?"

She appeared to roll her eyes, but it was hard to tell as her shawl had obscured my view of her face. I probably sounded like a typical tourist to her. "I love the mountains the most. But, these days, they are hard to enjoy."

I thought of the demons out there and wondered if that was what she meant. It had to be. "Why is it hard to enjoy the mountains? Is it the weather?"

"You wouldn't understand," she said, staring straight ahead.

Try me, I thought, but I decided not to press the issue. I didn't look like someone who had been alive for 2,000 years.

This young woman, too, was not all she seemed. Clearly, she had been ready for an attack when I approached her earlier. I would have loved to get a local perspective on the events taking place here. To do so would require some tact.

"I would love to buy you a coffee, as a thank you for helping me," I offered. "Since we're going to the same place, would you join me?"

Ileana shrugged her shoulder. "If you wish."

I hadn't expected her to agree so readily. Perhaps she would talk to me, after all. "Wonderful."

A few steps later, we were standing in front of a plain building made of ancient brick with the now familiar red roof. There was no signage. Nothing to indicate the name of the establishment, or if they were open or closed. Ileana opened the faded forest-green door and walked in ahead of me.

I never would have taken this building for a café. Nothing about the structure would have ever induced me to pull open the door. This seemed a sure-fire way to keep out non-locals. I followed her into a toasty warm space. The room was dimly lit with a smattering of small round tables covered in white lace tablecloths. People filled the room with lively chatter.

The aroma of coffee was a delight, and I thought of my flame-haired friend. Bria loved her coffee, which she used as fuel for many sleepless nights. Another pang of loneliness hit me. Before Bria, I was often alone, wandering the globe. I had grown used to her easy company, her sense of humor, and her heart. Alexandre, too, left a void. If I hadn't felt as if I was intruding on their budding relationship, I would have asked them to join me.

Of course, Bria was now out of demon-fighting commission for some time, so it was a good thing I hadn't. The last thing she needed was to travel, and the last thing I needed was to have a sick, pissed-off Bria on my hands.

A chair creaked along bare floorboards as Ileana pulled it out to sit. I mimicked her, dropping down across from the interesting young woman. Her face was youthful. She was no more than eighteen, I was sure. But her eyes spoke of age and experience. She had seen ugly things in life, I'd seen it time and again.

Before I could ask anything, we were joined by a middle-aged lady. She seemed tired with slumped shoulders and a shuffling gait. Wiry gray hairs were escaping her bun. She spoke in Romanian. Thankfully, Ileana took control. I hadn't bothered to learn the language, feeling I wouldn't be here long enough to make it worth my time.

"You only want coffee, yes?" she asked me.

When I nodded, Ileana answered the woman, who bustled off to the back.

I looked around, pretending to take in the room. What I was really doing was gathering my thoughts. I wanted to get what she knew out of her. I suspected she had knowledge of the demon activity, or she wouldn't have been so defensive in the street. Brasov didn't strike me as a violent place. "You defended yourself quite well out there. Is this a rough area of town?"

She looked at me, wariness in her eyes. "You have to be careful," was all she said with another shrug.

"Careful of the people?" I prodded. I couldn't let her off so easily. This was why I was here and the more she could tell me, the better.

"No, careful of the vampires." She rolled her eyes, leaning back in her chair. Her shawl fell away to reveal thick, dark hair. "Let me guess, you are here to see his castle. Most tourists are."

"Bran Castle? Honestly, I'm a little curious. But, I'm not a tourist. I'm here for work, researching local demon folklore for an article. Roll your eyes all you like." Bran Castle was the purported home of Vlad the Impaler, although there was no evidence he lived there. I had planned on visiting, once I was finished with the job. Who wouldn't want to take the opportunity to visit such an iconic location? What I could tell her about the man once he became immortal would no doubt amuse her.

Two steaming mugs of deep, black coffee were set in front of us by a young man whose eyes lingered on Ileana. The drinks smelled strong, earthy. I took the small, chipped mug in my hands, happy to have something to do.

Ileana didn't pay the young man any mind, and eventually, he walked away. She narrowed her eyes at me. "Demon folklore? Which demons are you studying?"

Since Whitby hadn't been specific, I improvised. As I rattled off some names, the last being martolea, Ileana squirmed in her seat. Her strength waned for the first time since our meeting. She was beginning to look a little uncomfortable as some of her bravado fell away.

"You must take care. Don't go out into the mountainside alone after dark." She looked at me intently, leaning forward in her chair. She replaced her scarf, draping it back over her head. Her face was that of a child. I wanted to protect her. I wanted to protect all these people who were trying to live their lives free of any struggle.

Still, if she had information, I needed it. "But I'm staying right in the mountains. I've taken a house in their very shadow. Are you telling me I'm not safe out there?"

Ileana sucked in her breath but didn't say any more. She crossed her arms and averted her eyes. Her body language made it clear she was hiding something.

"Is there something I should know, Ileana? Something you would like to tell me?"

"What? Do you want to hear crazy stories, so you can laugh at us back home?" she said this loudly, drawing looks from our neighbors.

I leaned forward, hoping to make her hear what I was really saying. "No, I would never laugh at you or anyone else. I think you would be surprised by what I believe. I may be able to help, if you would only open up."

I'd been told my demeanor and the softness of my voice could be calming, soothing to those in crisis. This young woman was not calmed by my words. In fact, she seemed to become more and more agitated. Ileana looked away, then jumped to her feet. "I have to go," she said as she bolted out the door.

I turned around in my seat, hoping to urge her back, but she was gone, the door swinging shut behind her. Great. Well, if I learned anything from this encounter, it was that the people here were scared. Hopefully, Ileana would stay out of harm's way until I could fully deal with the problem.

The people in the café were staring at me, probably wondering what I had said to upset their countrywoman. I laid several bills on the table, more than enough for two untouched coffees. I was eager to get on with this.

There were too many hours before dawn. I began to regret my agreement with Mr. Whitby to meet tomorrow night. The situation felt much more urgent.

I still needed to feed. Instead of taking a drink from Ileana, I found myself a lone male after exiting the café. The man was leaving his girlfriend's apartment, too inebriated to drive. I left him alive, but unconscious on the back seat of his car. He would sleep for a few hours, waking up with the sun.

Transylvania was an interesting place, so to kill time, I wandered the streets of Brasov. Most of the city was closed at this time of night. Not for the first time, I found myself wishing to peruse the shops and museums by day. I was envious of Alexandre for this; to be no longer bound by the night. The life of a vampire could be quite limiting when one could only function while the sun was down.

I walked farther into the city. Soon, I found myself at what must have been the center. From the rudimentary online search I did while in Paris, I knew this part of Brasov was called the Council Square. I walked the pedestrian-only street around the square, taking in the architecture. I was happy to find the place deserted. It wasn't quite spring, and the air was coldly crisp.

I spied a piece of paper lying on the edge of a large fountain. At first, I dismissed it as trash. As I drew nearer to the water, I saw it was a drawing.

I bent down for a closer look, spray from the fountain misting my face. It was a tarot card. The card was hand-drawn with obvious skill. The colors were bold, bright, the calligraphy of the words impeccable. The card was placed so that from my vantage point, it appeared upside down.

I straightened to look around. I was alone. Reaching over, I picked up the card and held it right-side up. *The Fool* was written along the bottom in looping scrolls. The card depicted a jester juggling balls over his head. Something compelled me to keep it, so I slipped it into the back pocket of my cotton pants.

I sat on a bench across from the feature, a formidable museum looming behind the sprays of water. The building was spotlit by the bright streetlights dotted around the square. The space was awash in artificial light. Water shot up and out from the center of the fountain, soothing me into a trance. It was nice to feel so relaxed.

That was, until I felt him. Not a demon this time. Something else entirely; a witch. I remained seated. The witch was behind me. I could feel him walking in an arc around me, giving me a wide berth. My skin tingled with the energy he gave off.

A.D. BRAZEAU

CHAPTER THREE

The witch appeared to the left of me, near the side of the fountain. I registered him out of the corner of my eye without moving my head. I didn't want to seem threatening, but I also wanted to have him in my sights.

"Are we going to have a problem?" he asked, his voice deep with an unmistakable southern accent. He stood still, not moving any closer.

"Depends on you," I answered, still as a statue.

"I'm cool if you are."

I inclined my head, my gaze never leaving the fountain. Did the witch leave the tarot card? I was hoping he would be on his way but couldn't be so lucky. He surprised me by moving closer until he was standing directly between me and the water. Maybe he was a threat.

The light was bright behind me, making it difficult to see him even with my preternatural eyes. He seemed to glow like fire in front of me.

"You know, there used to be a pillory in this square. It was used for punishments, humiliations, like they all were. It was also used for witches." His voice was low. Had there been any humans nearby, they wouldn't have heard him over the sound of the water. I could and he knew it.

"That's not surprising," I said. "Witches have been punished and much worse throughout human history, often for doing nothing at all."

"Indeed. Goodnight to you...bloodsucker." The witch inclined his head, leaving the way he came. It seemed Brasov was full of surprises.

The next night, it was time to meet my new employer. Mr. Whitby was a former Oxford professor of history who appeared to be a perennial bachelor.

I didn't know much about him. Usually, I tried to vet the people I worked with a little more thoroughly, but Whitby wasn't a digital kind of guy. A quick search on the internet hadn't led to much information. He had no social media presence, unusual for this day and age.

I did find two articles published by him during his tenure at Oxford. Both articles were on demon mythology. The topic of one, the Mbwiri of Central Africa and the other, the Yaoguai of China. Strange to find nothing published in his subject of history. Mr. Whitby seemed to have led a quiet life before coming to Brasov. The good thing was that he had no criminal record.

What led him here was unclear. I tried to never assume anything about anyone, but my guess was being a history professor with interests in demonology, he had come to this area for academic reasons. Whatever the case, I was soon to find out.

Mr. Whitby occupied the second floor above what appeared to be at one time another café. Unlike the place I visited with Ileana, this café had an old, weathered sign hanging above the door. The building was long closed, the windows shuttered with ancient, rotting wood.

A flash of color on the windowsill caught my eye. Unbelievable. I looked around. The street was deserted.

Another hand-drawn tarot card was placed upside down. This one read, *The Magician* and depicted a figure with one hand pointing to the sky and the other to the ground. What did this mean? Were they left for me or were they remnants of a superstitious people? I slid the card into my pocket, resolving to investigate this further.

I took the circular stairs on the side of the building two at a time, my long legs incapable of short strides. The door at the top of the staircase was propped open with a brick and the bergamot scent of freshly brewing Earl Grey wafted toward me.

I stood in the doorway, watching Mr. Whitby for a moment as he bustled around the small vintage kitchen, his back to me. This little apartment was no more modern than my rental cabin, but it appeared tidy from my vantage point. The yellow shag carpet was clean, and the grandma furniture wrapped in plastic covers was pristine.

"Knock, knock." I said the words as my knuckles lightly rapped on the door next to me.

Mr. Whitby jumped a little before turning with a laugh. "Dear me. I was expecting you, and yet you startled me. How silly I am. Come in, come in." Mr. Whitby was the quintessential professor. I liked him immediately. His white hair had cleared the top of his head, revealing a few liver spots. He wore wire-rimmed spectacles that did nothing to hide the warm sparkle in his eyes. I was sure the tweed jacket was an Oxford requirement.

"I'm so sorry I startled you." I moved into the tidy room. Everything was clean and welcoming, the kitchen table set for tea. I couldn't remember the last time I had tea; a century, at least.

"My fault entirely. It's a pleasure to meet you, Miss Selene." Mr. Whitby grasped my hand, warmly wrapping his free hand over both of ours. "Please sit. The tea is almost ready, then we can begin. It isn't civilized to have a discussion without tea."

I smiled, happy to oblige. What in the world did this sweet old man know about demons? He wasn't like any demon hunter I had ever known. I was still a bit on guard, but my instincts were telling me this man was harmless.

"Here we are." Mr. Whitby set the tea tray down on the little round table. The teapot was nestled in a homemade quilted tea cozy and there were little cakes, as well. "Please help yourself. I only stand on ceremony so far."

I poured out a cup of Earl Grey, leaving the cakes where they were. I took a sip of the steamy hot liquid before beginning. My curiosity over this man and his travels was overwhelming. "What brought you to Brasov, Mr. Whitby?"

"I am here on my sabbatical, studying demon folklore for a book I'm writing." He paused, taking a sip of his Earl Grey after adding a squeeze of fresh lemon to the top. "My interest here veered from the historical into what I once thought was the fantastical. Little did I know when I arrived, that a few months later I would actually encounter not only one demon, but several. It's a miracle I survived. These demons are becoming quite the problem here. Many locals can attest to this, although few will openly talk of it."

"Yes, I've noticed. The people here seem on their guard but won't say why."

Mr. Whitby nodded, continuing. "A band of folks goes out patrolling at night, hoping to run these creatures off. The men and women have yet to be successful. There aren't many of them, and they're untrained in fighting and weapons. I joined their ranks, hoping to be of some help while learning more about the infestation for my writing. But, really, none of us are equipped to deal with these beings. I'll admit I rather chickened out. Reading about such things is quite different than coming face-to-face with them. Milling about the internet one night, I ran into a chat board that spoke of you and the help you can offer people in similar circumstances. I didn't think it could hurt to contact you; one last effort before I leave this place."

I smiled, my fingers tracing the pattern on the teacup. "I'm glad you did. And how did you come across the Necromancy Wand?" This was a man who was previously untouched by the magical world. Coming into possession of such an item seemed impossible.

"I found it," he said simply.

"You found it," I repeated. How did someone outside of our world find an object of such power? My senses perked up.

"Yes, strange, isn't it? It was when I first arrived. I was exploring a castle not far from here. Actually." He shifted a little uncomfortably in his seat. "I wasn't supposed to be inside. I broke in, as it was. It's terrible, I know. I only wanted to be alone there, to poke about, if you will, without a spectator breathing down my neck. I meant no harm and I had this strange feeling that I couldn't shake. Down in the recesses, dungeons, if you like, I was doing some digging, illegal digging, and that was where I found it."

My eyes were wide. "Do you mean Bran Castle?" This small, proper man was illegally digging in Vlad the Impaler's dungeons? That was difficult to imagine.

"Yes, I know what you're thinking. I've never done anything like this, I swear. But something came over me. Something I can't explain. It was almost as if I was pulled by some unseen force. Of course, at the time I wouldn't have admitted that, but now, after all I've seen since then, I'm sure there was something else at work. Why I was meant to find the wand, I don't know. I've done a little research, but still, I am not sure what exactly it does. Until more can be learned, it's been tucked away out of sight. I thought someone like you, someone who lives in the world of demons all the time, may find the object useful. I suppose I was right."

He was more than right, still, I didn't want to seem too eager. Perhaps if I let on exactly how powerful this object was, he would increase his demands. Mr. Whitby didn't seem the type, but I'd been around long enough not to take people at face value. And what force was pulling him toward the wand, and why? It didn't make sense, not that anything magical ever did.

"I'll be happy to take it off your hands as soon as I fulfill your requirements. I'm ready to get started immediately."

"Oh, well, about that…" Mr. Whitby looked away, his hands fidgeting together. Here we go, I thought. What was he going to add to the deal?

I felt the atmosphere change behind me. There was an electrical charge in the air. Mr. Whitby's few hairs stood on end around his ears.

I didn't have to turn around to know who was there. A witch now loomed in the doorway, a witch I'd already encountered. What was going on here?

"Am I interrupting?" The voice was deep, smooth with a familiar southern accent. My stomach dropped. This couldn't be good. Twice in twenty-four hours was more than I'd been around a witch for ages. There was a reason for that.

Mr. Whitby clapped his hands together as he rose from his chair. "Wonderful. Now we shall have a proper introduction." He ambled over to the man in the doorway.

I had yet to turn around, my mind assaulting me with all manner of thoughts. Witches were rare these days. To come across a true witch was like finding a pot of gold at the end of a rainbow. Witches could be helpful in certain circumstances, but they usually had their own hidden agendas.

Reluctantly, I stood, turning to meet the newcomer. I was pretty sure whose face I was about to see.

"Who do we have here?" he drawled, moving toward me. He was a wonderful actor. Sweet Mr. Whitby would have no idea we'd spoken only last night.

"Tash Allerton, meet Selene," said Mr. Whitby, nervously messing with his few remaining hairs. This man was up to something.

"A pleasure, Selene. No last name?" asked Tash as we shook hands.

"Just Selene." I had no desire to get friendly with the man, but I also didn't want him to see my irritation.

"And what brings you here, just Selene?" Tash continued pumping my hand until I pulled it away.

Mr. Whitby cleared his throat. "Yes, well, I can explain everything. If you'll both sit down."

Tash and I eyed each other warily, each taking the measure of the other. He was as cautious of me as I was of him. Now that I could see him without the glare of the streetlight, he was rather nice to look at. Tash was attractive as men went; tall, obviously strong, and enough stubble to be considered roguish. If that was what he was going for. I made it a practice not to notice the opposite sex. I had too much to do, and they were a distraction I didn't need.

Tash spoke first. "Why is she here, Whitby? No offense, but I thought you and I were discussing business this evening."

"None taken, and I thought the same thing." I was here first, I thought. If this witch thought he was going to win my prize, it would be over my dead body. Tash slid his eyes toward me, then back to Mr. Whitby.

"Let me explain," began Mr. Whitby. "I felt the situation required some expeditiousness. To move things along more quickly, I thought a competition of sorts would be helpful."

"A competition." Tash and I repeated the word at the same time.

"Yes. Think of all this as a game. A most serious game. Winner takes all. In this case, the winner takes the wand. Simple." Whitby looked a little nervous as he addressed us, pressing his hands together a little too forcefully.

Simple. This was now anything but simple. Simple would have been to let me do my job. Now I had to worry about this witch and what he was going to do to win the prize. I may have had strength on my side, but he had deviousness. The wand was an object of immense power which I couldn't afford to allow into anyone else's hands. This job went from easy to complicated in the span of five minutes.

"Mr. Whitby, I think you're manipulating us," I said.

"Not at all, Selene. My only concern is the people of this city. I wish to see these awful demons rooted out, before it's too late. I am sorry if I've misled you. I only want this evil taken care of as swiftly as possible."

"Not a problem for me. These demons are as good as dead," Tash answered, puffing out his chest. Men. I didn't need to play peacock with him by inflating my physical body. He was no match for me.

I squared my shoulders, sitting as tall as I could. "Yes, they are. Because I'm going to finish them and take home the wand."

Tash smiled, his teeth perfect and dazzling. "May the best person win."

CHAPTER FOUR

Annoyed didn't begin to describe how I felt. A competition? I'd never heard anything so ridiculous in all my two thousand years. I wasn't about to hang around and make friends. Chatting over tea was not a good use of my time nor how I wanted to spend the evening. I needed the information on the demons causing the problems, then I was out of here.

"Why don't we get right into it, Mr. Whitby? What are we, I mean, what am I up against?" I crossed my arms, all business.

Mr. Whitby cleared his throat. "Indeed. I'm sure you are both eager to get out there." Mr. Whitby scooted his chair closer to the table. "Very well. There are two creatures wreaking havoc throughout the mountainside. The first are the varkolakas."

Mr. Whitby hadn't yet heard of my encounter outside of the little rental house. I saw no reason to tell him or Tash. They didn't need to know that not only had I already encountered a martolea, I had also bested him. I was sure these creatures would be on Whitby's list. How could they not be?

"Werewolves," I said for Tash's benefit. He was

squinting his eyes as though trying to figure out what Whitby was talking about. This guy was in way over his head. I stifled a laugh.

"Selene is correct. The varkolakas are not exactly what you're used to seeing in pop culture movies. This is not a classic wolfman or even a fully formed wolf. They are somewhere in between. Silver will burn it, but not kill it. Beheading should be your goal, although immolation will also work. The varkolakas are few. I believe at last count there was only a handful in the area, but you can imagine the problems they cause. They are large, strong, and merciless." Mr. Whitby looked at us for questions. I gestured for him to continue. I already knew all this. "Lastly, the strzyga."

Now he had my attention. The strzyga were vampiric creatures. It was my understanding they mostly kept to themselves. Hundreds of years ago, they were a force to be reckoned with; attacking travelers at night, sucking them dry. Kind of like other blood-drinking creatures I knew of. But they had been hunted to near extinction and were rarely heard of anymore. I had only ever seen them in drawings.

By all accounts, they were beautiful beings with the face, wings, and tail of an owl. Their arms and legs identified them as demons as they were bony and long, like those of an old crone.

"I thought the strzyga were no longer considered a threat. The few still in existence keep to themselves, feeding from wildlife." I thought it strange these creatures would suddenly become dangerous. And why had Whitby said lastly?

"Yes and no," answered Mr. Whitby. "They seem to be part of this new resurgence of demons, attempting to regain their status among the others and attacking human villagers."

Tash watched us, stroking his chin with his fingers. I didn't believe he knew what we were talking about. There was a compelling reason he wanted to get his hands on the wand. Something so important he was ready to fight demons for it; which I was sure he'd never done before. I would have to keep my eye on him.

Mr. Whitby was correct in that there had been a resurgence of demons worldwide. I had seen this firsthand over the last decade or so. Still, I wasn't sure about the strzyga. I would make the determination about them on my own.

"Any other questions?" Mr. Whitby looked from me to Tash.

"What about the martolea?" I asked. The time had come to confront this. I found it strange he never mentioned them. Clearly, they were also a problem.

Mr. Whitby resumed his seat across from me, waving his hand as if dismissing a thought. "I don't believe those creatures are much of a threat."

Not much of a threat? Tell that to the chunk of flesh torn from my shoulder. Had I been human, I may have bled out. Seemed like a threat to me.

Something was wrong. Those creatures were a problem, I'd bet my life on it.

"The martolea," continued Mr. Whitby, looking at Tash, "is a shapeshifting demon, although its size is limited. Rarely will you see a martolea in the shape of anything larger than say a wolf. Folklore says these beings once preyed solely upon women. Punishing them for doing work on the semi-holy day of Tuesday. Of course, this is nonsense. They attack both men and women and are not particular to any one day of the week. They are, however, terrifying in that they have a penchant for tearing out entrails."

"And shoulders," I said, my irritation beginning to show.

"What do you mean…shoulders." Tash stood with his hands on his hips.

"I lost a chunk from my shoulder to a martolea the night I arrived. I hadn't even gotten to my front door. Almost like he was waiting for me." I rubbed my arm, although by now it was healed. I left out my conversation with Ileana. They didn't need to know everything.

Mr. Whitby crossed his legs. "Most unusual. Perhaps this was an isolated incident. Keep your eyes open, of course, but I don't think it will be happening again."

"I assume they're killed in the usual ways?" Tash interrupted, still standing by the door. He was making his inexperience more and more clear.

"Yes, indeed. Piercing the heart, destroying the brain, or removing the head will work just fine. But, as I said, they shouldn't concern you like the other two," answered Mr. Whitby. "Any other questions for me?"

Tash shifted his weight from one foot to the other. I felt much satisfaction in watching him squirm a bit. He raised his hand like this was a classroom. "I have a few."

"I don't," I interrupted, pushing my chair back with a scraping sound. I wasn't usually so abrupt, but if this was a competition, I wasn't about to lose. "Good luck. I have a feeling you're going to need it." I patted Tash on the shoulder patronizingly as I began to walk out.

The situation was more complicated now. Working on my own would prove more time-consuming. I had no idea the magnitude of this witch's power. He was clueless about the demon realm, so that was helpful. This would matter little depending on his skill level.

The whole situation irritated me to no end. I walked through the streets of Brasov, my head down, my hands shoved into my pockets. I was sure the witch would have a whole host of tricks up his sleeve. I couldn't let him win the wand, whatever happened.

A partner was what I needed. Maybe I should bring Alexandre here after all. Bria would surely be fine for a few days.

I was walking with a little more force than I meant to, not paying attention to my surroundings. As I rounded the corner of a stone building that looked exactly like all the other buildings on this street, I ran smack into a body.

"Ow!" the body yelled as it flew backward, hitting the corner of the sidewalk with its rear end.

"I'm so sorry." I ran over, reaching down to assist the crumpled human. It was then I realized this was Ileana. Strange I should run into her again. I stood up straight, still looking down at her. "What are you doing out here? It's very late." I sounded more parental than I meant to, but this young woman should have been safe indoors.

"I could ask you the same question," she said, a testy bite to her voice. She stood, then leaned over to rub her backside. "Do you play American football? You're lucky you didn't break my tailbone."

I grimaced. "Yeah, sorry about that. I wasn't paying attention."

"Whatever. See you around."

I wanted to ask her to talk with me again. This wasn't the time, as she made clear. Right as Ileana was about to walk past me, we both heard it and froze. The low, deep growling was coming from about thirty feet in front of me.

I grabbed Ileana, spinning her behind me.

"What are you doing?" she protested.

"Saving your life. Run and get to cover now." I moved into a fighting stance, facing the shadows ahead. There was movement as the demon was readying to pounce.

"You run and get to cover," said Ileana as she stepped alongside me, her arms raised in a defensive position.

My mouth fell open. Although her posture could use improvement, she appeared to have some training. I wanted to question her but there was no time. Two martolea had us in their sights. I knew these beasts were a problem. Why had Mr. Whitby insisted they were not? All I had on me was a dagger sheathed in a holster underneath my shirt. Ileana didn't appear to have any weapons.

I couldn't let myself worry about her. If she wanted to fight, that was her choice. I could not be distracted. With vampiric speed, I pulled out my tactical knife, silver metal flashing in the shine from the streetlamp.

As I did so, the two martolea moved from the shadows into the light. The form they had taken was disturbing; each creature had the head and upper body of a black wolf with satyr-like hind legs. This afforded them the opportunity to attack with their front legs drawn up like arms.

Ileana took a step back. As much as I couldn't let her distract me, I did hope she would run to safety. The martolea, at first standing side by side, broke off from each other.

One headed straight for me, the other for Ileana. There was no stopping what she was about to see. This problem had only one solution.

Rather than wait for mine to descend upon me, I closed the distance with preternatural speed. I meant to sink my dagger into the demon's skull, but it dodged me, and I crashed into the back end of a parked car, moving it forward by about ten feet.

I pushed myself off the metal bumper, now dented by my hip. I spun around, fear spiraling through my gut as I saw both demons descend upon Ileana.

The girl was flexible. She landed an impressive kick in the solar plexus of one, which momentarily sent it back a few paces.

Unfortunately, her moves weren't enough to keep them both back for long. The wolf-satyr who had dodged me was on top of her in her a heartbeat, pinning her arms to the pavement, teeth snarling inches from her face. Ileana thrashed and kicked to no avail.

I pushed myself forward, launching my body into the side of the demon as it was widening its mouth to take a bite. Saliva dripped down onto Ileana's cheeks as she fought to push it off.

The creature yipped as I barreled into it, smashing its body into the street, bits of fur and skin left in our wake. Pinning the monster's chest under my knee, I plunged my knife into its eye socket, burying the dagger up to the hilt.

The martolea twitched once beneath me and vanished

into the mist. Behind me, I heard a gasp. I expected to see Ileana half-eaten. I was surprised to instead see her wrestling on the ground with the other demon. She was doing a decent job, the only problem being she didn't have a weapon to finish it off. I dashed over and plunged my dagger into its temple. Her eyes went wide as the demon disappeared like smoke.

"You have skills," I said, impressed. I hoped she hadn't noticed my speed, but she had.

Ileana backed off from me, moving backward down the street. She raised a hand, pointing a finger at me. "You're strigoi. That's why you were stalking me last night. You were going to drink my blood. Stay away from me, beast."

"Ileana, wait. Please stop and talk with me. I wasn't going to hurt you. I just saved you." I gestured to the air in between us, attempting to make my point with nothing to show for it. "I'm here to help, with all of this. Maybe we could work together."

She stopped at this. "Help you? How? I won't bring you people to feed on if you're looking for an Igor."

I shook my head. "Different movie. I'm not a threat to the people here. I'm going to take care of your little demon problem and move on. Another pair of hands, someone who knows the area and superstitions, would be most helpful. You've dealt with demons before, haven't you? No doubt you could tell me a story or two."

"Why help us?" She hadn't moved, and I hoped she was at least considering my request. The young woman was interesting. She could handle weirdness and she could fight.

"Because this is what I do. I travel all over the world helping people like you."

"A strigoi... helps people."

"Yes." I chuckled. "I'll leave you for the night. The last thing I want to do is frighten you. But please think on what I've said. If you'd like to team up, meet me here tomorrow night." With that, I jumped to the nearest rooftop. I could have walked down the street, but felt a little display was in order. My hope was after the fight and the theatrics, she would see I could be a formidable ally.

I thought more on Mr. Whitby and his insistence that these creatures were not a threat. Was he lying? Or did he not know any better? He was new to all this. I would give him the benefit of the doubt for now, but I would watch my back very closely.

CHAPTER FIVE

Connecting with strong females seemed to be what I did best. My mother was the strongest female I'd ever known. I tried to follow in her footsteps as much as I could but felt like I never really lived up to her legend. The real-life story of Cleopatra, a woman who dominated men and ruled a powerful country in a time when women were subservient, was a lot to live up to.

Bria was also strong. Even with the strength of a human, she could kick some demon butt, readily accepting the possible consequences. Not only was she physically strong, but emotionally, as well. She had been through a lot, and nothing could break her.

I could sense the same strength in Ileana. She may not have been quite the physical badass Bria was, but if she kept at it, her skills would develop over time. I felt it imperative to get a weapon in that young woman's hands.

After roaming over the rooftops of Brasov, I returned to the cabin to regroup. I didn't have the luxury of time. Not only were the demons here getting too friendly with the town, the witch was vying with me for the wand. There was still a long way to go until dawn, and there was no way I could sit and wait. The time to act was now.

I didn't want to think much yet on the strzyga. The martolea should be my first target, regardless of what Whitby said. They were a pain, but other than the shapeshifting, there wasn't much to them. The creatures were easily handled by an immortal as long as this immortal didn't have to face too many at once.

The one question which gave me pause was how many were out there? And why was Whitby not concerned with them? I had seen those creatures twice now, and I'd barely arrived in Brasov.

Despite this, I decided to work this evening on the varkolakas. If there was only a handful, maybe this was my place to start. It seemed strange I hadn't heard of them causing problems on the internet. Typically, when weres were involved, people became interested in a hurry.

The isolation of the cabin provided me enough cover from mortals. Not only the location but the time of night would also help keep my activities from prying eyes.

Digging through my weapons trunk, I pulled out what I would need. I strapped a holster for a dagger around my right thigh. My katana was securely buckled across my back. I still had the dagger under my shirt and thought this would be adequate. With two hands, I could only hold so much and didn't want to be too weighed down.

My mind clear and focused on werewolves, I strode out the front door. The weres would keep to the deeper mountain areas, so that was where I headed.

The forested mountains were beautiful. I could see why hikers sought these peaks. There was green all around. The pine and fir trees created a wonderland that smelled of Christmas while the ash and beech trees filled the space with dewy, green leaves. A small rivulet of water trickled down the mountain alongside the path I walked. This was a charming fairytale place. I would make it safe for nature lovers once again.

A rustling sound startled me from my reverie.

"Whoa, that's some weapon you've got there. I see we

had the same idea. Great minds must think alike." The deep voice came from behind.

I stopped, put my hands on my hips, and slumped my head forward. I thought of how best to deal with this situation. "Yes, I suppose so," I said, turning toward Tash. "But, as you can see, nothing is out here. I was just about to head back to town."

"Were you?" Tash narrowed his eyes. He wasn't buying it.

I nodded my head, hoping he would take my word for it. "It's a no-go. I've been out here for over an hour, and—nothing. Besides, no full moon, so no werewolves." I pointed up to the sliver of moon, barely visible off in the distance over the treetops.

He looked up at the sky, then back to me, a scowl on his face.

"Now, I know you're pulling my leg. I'm not a complete idiot. I do know the full-moon thing is a myth. Mostly because Whitby told me, but still. Plus, there are also the owly vampires to consider. I'll hang out a while longer. It could be you haven't been looking hard enough."

And now, I wanted to punch him.

I thought maybe I could trick Tash with the full moon, but no dice. For a moment, I considered sharing with him my concern over the martolea and the strzyga.

One look at his face wiped the thought from my head. His eyes were focused, his brow knit together. He was ready to hunt some demons. What was this guy's deal? Witches usually steered clear of this kind of trouble. They were better suited to dark rooms and brewing cauldrons.

I knew better than to trust people, especially witches and especially men. He would prove no different than any other man I'd ever known. Attractive though he may be.

I supposed my lack of trust in the male sex came from my mortal life. As a child, Marc Antony would leave Egypt to return to Rome and his Roman wife Octavia, leaving Mother in fits of rage. Her pain would last for weeks after.

She was deeply hurt every time he left. Later, my deep seated fear and distrust of Octavian led to nightmares from which I would wake screaming. He was never to be trusted, not even once I'd grown and gone to live in my new home. My mortal husband was kind enough, though I never believed him truly faithful. Alexandre was the first man in two millennia to surprise me.

My attention moved back to the witch. Tash was dressed in formfitting black jeans, a black sweater, and worn-looking motorcycle boots. His camouflage was working well for him, except for one thing. I turned my head and had a laugh at his expense.

"What's so funny?" There was a testiness to his voice.

I stopped my snickering long enough to say, "You may want to consider wearing a cap over your head."

Tash's hand went over his round head. "Why?"

"There's a glare off your bald dome." I found men with shaved and bald heads attractive, and he was no exception. I wouldn't have told him this in a million years, but Tash also had the deep-brown soulful eyes and perfectly groomed goatee of one of my favorite actors.

He pulled a face and yanked a knit cap out of the back pocket of his jeans. "Very funny," he said.

I shrugged. "You don't want to give the demons any more advantages than they already have. A werewolf will pull you limb from limb without even breaking a sweat." I paused as we walked along, to watch him as I said this.

He swallowed hard. "How many werewolves have you fought? Any tips for a newbie?" If he wasn't a witch and we weren't in a competition for something very precious, I would have felt sorry for him.

I hadn't come across many werewolves in all my long life and had only ever seen the result of one were attack. This did lead me to wonder how deadly and prevalent they could be. But Tash didn't need to know that. "Enough to know you're too green for this. You shouldn't be here."

"I have to be here." There was an edge to his voice that

gave me pause as he continued walking.

I planted my feet firmly into the forest floor. "Why? Why do you seek the wand?"

"My reasons are mine alone. Don't worry about me, I'll be fine." Tash met my eyes and for a second, something almost stirred inside me for this strange witch.

I doubted he would be fine but couldn't take on the responsibility of worrying about his welfare. "I'm sure you will be. Seriously, though. I don't think it's a good idea for us to hunt together. We're in a competition. A competition I intend to win. So, if you don't mind, I'll head this way. You should take your broom and head that way." I pointed to our right.

"You're full of jokes, aren't you? Are we going to talk about the fact that you're a vampire?" He came to a stop. As he did so, he laid a hand on my arm—the energy was palpable, and it wasn't malicious. I shook it off. I would not allow myself to feel anything for him.

I knew he could tell what I was, the same as how I'd felt what he was at the fountain. I held up my head. "What about it?"

"Whitby doesn't know, does he?" Tash smirked in a way that made me want to slap him.

"No. Did you tell him?"

"I didn't. There's no reason I should tell a secret that doesn't belong to me."

"Thanks for that. I'd like to keep Whitby in the dark. He's new to all this and my vampirism would spook him."

Tash nodded. "Sure, I don't mind keeping your secret. But don't forget I'm doing you a favor."

I narrowed my eyes. Exactly like a witch. I silently thanked this man for reminding me I couldn't trust him as far as I could throw him. "Just stay out of my way." I turned on my heel, striding up the mountain path. The farther Tash the witch stayed away from me, the better.

Fuming, I walked further up the mountain. I let Tash

infect my thoughts so deeply, I almost didn't hear them. Stopping, I looked up. Perched on the branch of an oak tree sat two strzyga. Their breath was soft as they watched me with their wide, beautiful eyes.

They were both female, their owl-like faces framed by dark, long flowing hair. Their enormous wings were tucked around their bodies. Each was clutching the branch they sat on with spindly, crone-like arms. They were full-grown. I suspected were they to stand straight, they would have been around five feet tall.

I sensed no malice from them, only curiosity. Their liquid eyes blinked open and closed. They surely knew what I was. What was I supposed to do? Attack these creatures? They were no threat to me. I had a hard time believing they were a threat to anyone.

"Hello," I ventured.

The one closest to me tilted her head with a ripple of downy feathers. I wasn't sure if she was trying to communicate or merely taking my measure.

I stood in a relaxed stance, my arms down at my side. "You're not really attacking the village, are you?"

She tilted her head to the other side, then shook it from left to right.

"There's a man who wishes you to be exterminated. Do you know why?"

Again, the head moved from left to right. I sighed. I wouldn't be able to get any useful information from these beings communicating like this.

If my history was correct, according to Romanian mythology, the strzyga were born human with two hearts and two souls. After the mortal soul passed, one would remain behind, turning into a vampire owl that would drink the blood of those who traveled at night. This was undoubtedly true. Most vampires attacked and killed humans at random long ago.

Only in recent times did they learn to be a little more discerning. I suspected the same was true for these creatures. Although they couldn't or wouldn't speak, they appeared to be intelligent. I would need more time to consider my options.

"There is another who is out to hunt you. Please do me a favor and flee as far as you can for the time being and keep out of sight. I'm going to figure this out but need time. Do you understand?"

The feathered face nodded once then took flight with her companion. I watched them go, marveling at how graceful they were for such large beings. What a shame it would be to see them extinct. Why was I really brought here? Things were beginning to feel even stranger than usual. One thing was for sure, I would get to the bottom of this.

A.D. BRAZEAU

CHAPTER SIX

As dawn was fast approaching, I made my way back to my rustic shelter. I thought of Tash and wondered how he fared out on the mountain, alone. If he was unlucky enough to find a werewolf or two, I doubted it would go well for him.

I didn't trust him. Before I could form a plan as to what I would say, my phone was out. I touched Whitby's name and the other end began to ring. This was probably a bad idea.

"Hello, this is Joseph Whitby." He answered as I would expect any proper Englishman to.

"Mr. Whitby, this is Selene."

"Oh, yes, my dear. I was distracted and didn't look before I answered. How can I be of service?" He did seem distracted. I caught a sound in the background that sounded like scuffling but couldn't make it out.

"Well, I have a couple of things I'd like to discuss with you. First, I believe you've made a mistake about the strzyga. Those beings are no danger to anyone, Mr. Whitby. They need to be struck from your list. I'm really quite worried for their welfare."

Whitby mumbled something which sounded like a

dissent. "I see. Are you sure they haven't tricked you in some way, Selene? Even me, as inexperienced as I am, know how insidious these creatures can be."

"I'm positive. They wouldn't hurt a fly. I can see why they would be frightening to any humans who came across them, but I assure you, they are no danger. Probably haven't been for hundreds of years."

There was a pause on the other end. "If you say so, Selene. You are the expert, after all. What else did you want to talk with me about?"

I took a moment to consider how I would frame this. I didn't want to sound like I was tattling. I thought of Bria and Alexandre when they first met. One would often tattle on the other. "I'm concerned about the witch. Since arriving in Brasov, I've found two tarot cards. I can't be sure they were left specifically for me. However, it does seem odd. Tarot cards are something witches utilize often."

There was another shuffling sound in the background. Whitby must have been pacing his apartment.

"Interesting. I've wondered about him myself; truth be told. Witch, you say? I'd no idea. Goodness, the things I'm learning. He came to me. Somehow, he knew I possessed the wand."

The momentary discomfort I felt at outing Tash as a witch disappeared at this news. What was Tash Allerton really doing here? "I'll be on my guard. You, sir, should be, as well."

"This is all quite strange for me, Selene. Do you think we're in danger?"

"From Tash? I'm not sure. If anything else comes up, I'll let you know." I ended the call with Whitby. This was uncomfortable. Tash had approached Whitby? How on earth did he know about the wand? He seemed pretty clueless about demons in general.

I massaged the back of my neck. This was beginning to be more complicated than I had originally assumed. I hated the thought of doing this alone.

I slipped through the front door as the sky was beginning to lighten. I locked the door, then pushed the couch in front of it for good measure. The sheets on the twin bed were almost threadbare but felt like heaven, nonetheless. It had been one long night of some interesting twists and turns. Nothing was ever simple, and nothing was ever as it seemed. Even after 2,000 years on this earth, I could still be surprised.

Scratching on the front door pulled me from sleep. For a moment, I froze under the sheets, unsure what sort of creature had come knocking. I groaned a little, not quite ready to peel myself out of bed. Vampires had moments of laziness, too. The events of the night before left me unsure I wanted to be here.

More scratching propelled me to my feet. I rubbed at my eyes as I walked to the door. The scent of a chai latte and human perked me up and I realized the person on the other side of the door was Ileana.

"I thought I said to meet me in town," I said as I unceremoniously kicked the couch out of the way and pulled open the door. "Besides, how did you know where to find me?"

"Good evening to you, too," she said, holding out a disposable cup of happiness, which she then retracted. "Can you even drink this? I guess I wasn't thinking."

I smiled, realizing I sounded grumpy. "Sorry, it was a long and weird night. And, yes. Yes, I can."

"What could possibly be weird about Brasov?" joked Ileana, placing the cup in my eager hand. "To answer your question, my uncle was your driver. He has had a lot of choice things to say about the tourist with the heavy trunks. He wasn't happy about having to lash them to the top of his car."

I shook my head, laughing. "I've no doubt. But I couldn't very well sling them around myself. It would be a dead giveaway to what I am."

I stood back for her to enter. As I did so, my gaze fell on the chair outside. If I had a working heart, it would have stopped.

"What the hell?" I stepped outside to look down at the tarot card. This one matched the others with the same exquisite drawing and coloring. It was *The High Priestess* and was to my vantage point, again upside down. I recognized my mother goddess. The card depicted Isis as The High Priestess standing between two columns with an ankh worn around her neck.

"What?" Ileana popped her head out the door.

"Did you leave this here?" I pointed down to the card, almost afraid to touch it.

She stepped out and looked down. Ileana shook her head. "No. I hate those things."

I moved out in front of the little house, my senses on high alert. Save for a few owls and other harmless animals, there was no one about but us.

Snatching up the card, I motioned to the door. "Let's go inside."

I left Ileana in the dining area and went to lay the card with the others on the dresser, *The Fool, The Magician,* and now *The High Priestess* depicted as Isis. This was now officially creepy. The whole thing had a very witchy vibe.

Ileana was standing awkwardly where I had left her. I sensed doubts about being here swirling around her mind. "Please sit down," I offered.

She hesitated, looking back at the bedroom. "What does the card mean?"

"I've no idea." I sighed. "But I intend to find out. It's the third such card I've found since arriving in town. I know about as much as you do about tarot. Please." I gestured to the small dining set.

Ileana wiped off one of the dining chairs with her bare hand before sitting. "Someone's warning you, maybe. Or, threatening you. You should look up their meaning."

She was right. The cards could mean anything. "I'll do

that, after we chat."

Ileana nodded, taking a sip of her drink. "Let's talk more about what you are. I realize you are strigoi. But you are in no way what I thought a strigoi was."

I pulled out a chair opposite her. "I can only imagine what you thought we were like. I'm guessing monstrous, with pale skin, bloody fangs, and long pointy nails."

Ileana unwound her pale pink headscarf, settling it around her shoulders. "Something like that. Instead, your skin is a golden brown, I don't really see any fangs, and your nails are neat and manicured. Add to that your killing of demons, overall gentle demeanor, and yoga instructor look. Boy, did we have it wrong."

I laughed, looking down at my tunic and leggings. "They weren't always wrong. My kind have evolved into what we are now. Back in the days when the myth of the strigoi was created, those creatures were no doubt vicious and bloodthirsty. I've known a few like that, even in modern times. A lot of it has to do with what a person was like as a human. If you're a crappy human, you'll be a crappy immortal, too." I tried to keep my face warm, my movements slow. She may have accepted what I am, but that didn't mean I couldn't spook her. I wanted her to be as comfortable with me as possible.

Ileana crossed her legs, her hands wrapped around her warm cup. "What are you doing here? You said you were here to help. Is this true?"

"It's true. Fighting demons is kind of my thing. You could help me a great deal by telling me more about your experiences with the demons of Brasov. What can you tell me about the strzyga and varkolakas?" I sipped on the delicious chai. Although vampires could not ingest solid food, we could handle liquids other than blood on occasion.

"The what?" Ileana looked at me with blank eyes.

Perhaps she didn't know the proper names. "Strzyga are owl-like vampiric beings. They can fly and resemble large owls with human-like arms and hair. Varkolakas are basically werewolves."

She tilted her head, a puzzled look on her face. "That's what attacked us last night? The dogs were werewolves?"

"No, those were martolea. They're shapeshifting demons. The form they chose last night was half-satyr, half-wolf. A true werewolf is much larger, and although they can walk on two legs, those legs are wolf-like, not satyr-like. The martolea will also appear as a large dog. I was attacked by one of those the moment I arrived." Ileana's response was confirming something I was already beginning to suspect. The only problem here was the shapeshifters. Why would Whitby send us on a wild goose chase? Maybe he didn't even realize his error.

"Then those are the demons that are plaguing us; the martolea. Strzyga sound familiar, but I haven't heard of them bothering anyone. I've only read about them in books." Ileana took a drink of her chai.

"Tell me more about your experience with the martolea. Have you been attacked before?"

She shook her head, her scarf billowing around her shoulders. "No. It started with a boy I went to school with. He was hiking in the mountains last summer. His body was found days after he went missing. It was...torn to shreds. Unlike anything anyone here had ever seen. The attack was blamed on a pack of ravenous wolves, tragic, but one of those things that happen from time to time.

"A few weeks later, a group of tourists was attacked hiking in the same area. There were four of them. These were all large, strong men. They barely fought off the attack. One of the men lost his arm. In the hospital, these men told a tale, not of wolves, but of beasts. They were wolf and goat combined. The men were laughed at. The authorities assumed they were drinking or on drugs. The police went out to eliminate the wolf pack causing the trouble. Only, they too met with an attack they couldn't fully explain. One of the officers died. Superstitious gossip spreads quickly here. Within days, a group of vigilantes formed with the purpose of putting down what many were now calling demons. Since then, two more have been killed and several injured. Not even one of the beasts has been put down, to my knowledge. They are too strong, too fast. I decided to learn some defensive moves and began taking lessons from a karate instructor who lives next door." Ileana shivered. She set down her chai, running her hands over her upper arms to warm herself.

I sat thinking for a moment. How much should I share with this young woman? I wanted to tell her everything but wasn't sure how much she was ready for. She had taken in a lot already.

I set down my cup and propped my elbow on the table. "Okay, then I'll focus my efforts on the martolea."

"Focus your efforts?" she asked, shifting a bit in her seat.

"Yeah. I'm pretty sure the others are no threat and I will do my best to prove that." I thought of the witch and let out an exasperated sigh. "I need to tell Tash, so he doesn't go off half-cocked and kill a bunch of innocent creatures. Although, there's no proof the werewolves are innocent yet."

"Who's Tash? Your partner?"

I blurted out a laugh. "No. I'm partner-less now. He's here to hunt the same demons."

"Just not with you."

"Right. Not with me. This is becoming more complicated than I thought." I drummed my fingers on the table, considering my next move.

"Well, you're not partner-less. I'm going to help you," Ileana said, resolution in her voice.

I smiled. I could use the help. Ileana would be a wonderful asset in the research department. I wanted her safely behind closed doors, not out hunting for vicious shifter-dogs.

"We have a lot to do. Are you able to be away from home in the evenings? And will our nights affect what you do during the day? If you have a boyfriend, this might be hard to explain." I thought of the boy eyeing her in the café. If she was still living at home, I imagined that too would be a little difficult for her.

"I'm a lesbian. And I'm single. So, no worries there. I have my own apartment above my parents' shop. No one will notice my coming and going. I work remotely for an IT company during the day, so if I get my work done, it's all good. I'm saving for college. One more year of working full-time and I should have the first half paid for," she said proudly, a smile on her face.

Ileana was impressing me more and more. She was tech-savvy, hard-working, and smart. We could accomplish much together.

"Perfect. Then the first thing I need to do is find Tash. I'm going to set you up here with my texts. We need to find out more about these demons of Brasov, particularly the martolea."

Ileana didn't look pleased. "That doesn't sound like much of a partnership. It sounds like I'm working for you."

"I understand, but we need more information. As soon as I talk with Tash, I'll head back here, and we can regroup. It's all hands-on-deck."

She sighed and shrugged her shoulders. "All right. Only don't make it a habit to leave me out."

I agreed. I had something else to say as I pulled out the trunk of magical books. "As my partner, you should know that I don't trust Tash. I'm not sure if I can trust Whitby, either. He's the guy who brought me here. They both seem to be hiding things. This doesn't necessarily mean one of them intends harm. I'll start with Tash, innocently asking for help to figure out what's up with Whitby. Then, I'll slip in the cards and see what his reaction is." I paused, pinching the bridge of my nose between my fingers. There was so much to explain. "You should know Tash is a witch. The situation here is complicated, like I said, and we'll have to navigate it the best we can."

"A witch." Ileana shook her head. "I guess if I can deal

with a strigoi, I can deal with a witch. Can he put a spell on me?"

"Actually, he can. I doubt he would have any reason to, though."

I pushed the lid of the trunk open. Ileana seemed to be amazed at all the books, carefully pulling them out one a time and laying them on the floor around her. Pretty soon, she was surrounded by volumes of all kinds. "No wonder this trunk was so heavy," she said with a laugh.

We were looking for anything relating to the martolea; weaknesses were especially helpful. After I had given her instructions on what to look for and where to start, I grabbed the cards. I headed out to find Tash, wondering if he was behind the mysterious deck of tarot I was slowly being fed.

Being able to feel a witch, I knew I could find him if he was relatively close. The cold night air would have raised goosebumps had I been mortal. As it was, the coolness felt good to me. The sky was clear overhead, helping to light my way to town. All was quiet except for the nightly choir of hooting owls.

The moment I arrived on the outskirts of the little European city, I reached out with my mind. To a vampire, a witch would feel almost like an electrical zap. I walked down the center of a deserted cobblestone street, endless row homes in front of me, the sharp fresh smell and sound of running water from a nearby fountain drawing my attention. I tried to feel the witch but also kept an eye out for the Hounds of Hell.

Turning onto the next street, I jumped as if I had stuck my finger in a power outlet. "There you are," I said to myself. I followed the feeling, the hairs on my arms standing on end until I came to a dark alleyway. I looked up and noticed the light from the streetlamp was out. I was sure this was the witch's doing. Why did he want to be in the dark? To see who was coming, have the advantage?

I stood still, looking around. There was an open window

to my right, all the way at the dead end of the alley. Not only were the hairs on my arm and the back of my neck standing at full attention, but I could also smell something like bitter herbs. I pictured a cauldron filled with a mysterious, bubbling concoction. It was pointless to stalk the night when he could feel me out here.

A minute later and I was knocking on a door with no number.

"Let me guess who that is," rumbled a voice from the other side.

I did nothing to wipe the sour look off my face as Tash let me in. I refused to notice how good he looked in skin-tight black jeans and a black t-shirt that showed every defined muscle from his shoulders down to his waist. "What stinks? Please don't tell me that's your dinner." I was generally a sweet person, but there was something about this man that made me crazy.

"Hungry? Oh, right, you don't eat and I'm fresh out of blood."

"No, you're not." I crossed my arms, turning narrowed eyes on him.

Tash made a stab at mock laughter, which ended up sounding more like a dying cow. "Okay, what do you want? I would invite you in to sit down, but I'm guessing you're here for a specific reason and not a social call."

"Actually, I'd love to sit. We have some important things to talk about. Things that concern us both and why we're here." I looked around the small front room. His accommodations were not any better than mine. I helped myself to a poorly painted orange chair by the open window.

Tash sighed, shutting the door after realizing I wasn't going anywhere. He walked closer but remained standing. He made a *go on* gesture with his hands, not bothering to use actual words.

I dove right in. "We have a problem with Whitby. I can't be sure, but I think there's something very wrong here."

CHAPTER SEVEN

"What do you mean, something is wrong here?" Tash remained standing in front of me, one arm wrapped around his stomach, the other propping up his chin.

I didn't trust the witch, but I also didn't want him out there killing innocent beings. I had to figure out what was wrong and working with Tash, or pretending to, seemed to be my only option. I wasn't any good at deception and half-truths.

I chewed on the inside of my cheek, figuring out how to frame my thoughts. "Whitby said the varkolakas and the strzyga are the demons causing problems in Brasov. Only, I know one of the locals. She had no idea what those demons even are. The issues here are being caused by the martolea."

"Which Whitby denied being a concern." Tash took a seat across from me, elbows resting on his knees. He was catching on fast.

"Exactly. I've already had two run-ins with them." It wasn't until my shoulders relaxed that I realized how tense I was. Who was to say if Tash would even listen to me? He wanted the wand. Would he go to any lengths to get it? Even if it meant killing innocent creatures?

Tash looked away, toward the window. I let my

revelation hang in the air for a minute, wanting and hoping Tash would come to the same conclusion I had. I reminded myself that he approached Whitby and not the other way around. I was walking a fine line here.

He turned his face back toward me. "What do you know about Whitby?"

"Not much. I probably know as much as you do; he's an Oxford professor here in Romania doing research for a book. He contacted me through a chat board, which isn't unusual. The thing is, I don't sense anything off about him. I almost wonder if he's being used by someone else or maybe he's so ignorant about demons he really has no clue as to what is happening here." Tash could be the one using the professor. If so, I was playing my hand all wrong.

Tash made a face. "Possibly. Our world is a unique one. The learning curve is long. Do you buy his story about how he came across the wand?"

I shrugged, crossing one leg over the other. "You said it yourself. Our world is a unique one. The Necromancy Wand is a magical object. If it wanted to be found on that day, it would make sure it was. There isn't anything unusual about magical objects suddenly appearing out of nowhere and finding their way into the hands of a human."

"That's certainly true." Tash leaned back, his eyes never leaving my face. "So, does this mean you want to work with me?"

"I don't know what options we have right now. A semi-partnership may be helpful until we know for sure what gives. I'm worried about the strzyga. They're harmless, gentle beings. I need your word that you will leave them alone. The jury's out on the werewolves until I see them for myself."

He considered me for a moment, his gaze penetrating mine. "Trusting a vampire is not something I would have thought I'd ever do. Our kinds don't exactly mix well." Tash had an edge to his voice which annoyed me.

"No kidding. How do you think I feel? Witches are the

least trustworthy creatures on the planet." I folded my arms across my chest. I was beginning to wonder how much time I'd wasted in this crummy apartment. The truth was; I had worked with witches in the past. The long-ago past and never for any great length of time. They were useful, but dangerous. They always wanted a little more than I was willing to give.

"Witches aren't trustworthy? How many have you actually known?" Tash wasn't backing down.

He had a point. "A couple." Truth be told, I have found the witches I worked with to be quite effective and helpful, but he was right, we don't mix well. Probably because not only do they always seem to want a piece of your soul, when you put two different kinds of powerful beings in the same room, egos will often get in the way.

"If you want an opinion from a witch's perspective; vampires are the untrustworthy ones. My kind have had to protect ourselves from vampires who would try and drain us for our powers for millennia." He shifted in his seat. "I've heard several tales of witches who were turned by their immortal captives, only to be hunted down and exterminated by other witches for fear they would become a powerful abomination."

I rolled my eyes. I was so tired of hearing about the vampires of old and all their misdeeds. "And how old were these tales you've heard? My guess is very. These things simply don't happen in modern times. Witches, too, have been known for dark deeds."

"Prejudices are hard to get rid of." There was something so simple and heartrending about this statement that I stopped feeling derisive all at once.

"You're right. So, let's get rid of them and help each other. At least so far as to figure out what is going on. Then, if we get this straightened out, we go back to competing for the wand."

Tash nodded his head. "Deal." He stuck out his hand, which I grasped. He agreed a little too easily.

"What do you want with the wand, anyway?" I didn't think he would answer but couldn't help but ask.

Tash's dark eyes became darker for one fleeting moment. "I want to add it to my collection of magical objects. Probably the same as you."

We had just talked about the thousands of years of bad blood and prejudice between our kinds. I wanted to believe we could move past all that. But there was something off about his answer. He was clearly hiding something. I knew there was more to it than that. It didn't matter, since I was the one who would be leaving Romania with the wand, but I still wanted to believe he could be trusted.

"How did Whitby find you?" I asked, hoping he would give more insight into who he was, and to see how he would lie.

"Through my website." Usually, I could tell when someone was telling me a lie. This man should have been a professional poker player.

"You have a website?" I wondered what a witch's website would consist of.

Tash laughed. "I do. It's a new age, isn't it? I offer services, spells and such. It's mostly a rip-off. When people ask for love spells, the most popular request by far, I send them a vial of tap water and tell them to have the object of their affection drink it. On occasion, I get a request for something valid, like a cure for an illness. I do what I can to help." He shrugged. "It's a living. A far cry from my ancestors who died in Salem, among other places, for being themselves."

He had a point. There was no longer any shame in calling oneself a witch. Of course, most of the public doesn't realize there are witches with actual powers, so that made a difference. Vampires, on the other hand, would likely never be able to live in the open. We would always be relegated to nightmares and shadows.

"What do you know about tarot cards?" I asked, watching him intently for any sign he was telling me more lies.

"Everything, I'm a witch. Why?" He continued to look at me with the same unwavering expression. He was good.

"Since arriving in Brasov, I have found three hand-made tarot cards. All at different times, in different locations."

"And you think they were left for you? It's not a coincidence? This is a superstitious place."

I nodded, a chill spiking its way down my spine. The cards were no coincidence. *The High Priestess* card left on my porch confirmed this.

Tash's brow crinkled. He looked away for a moment as if to catch a thought. "Do you have them?"

I pulled the three cards from my pants pocket and handed them toward Tash. He held up his hands like this was a hold-up and pointed to the coffee table.

"Lay them down exactly as you found them, in order. I can't touch them yet."

I wondered why. If he placed a spell on them, would something happen if he touched them? I did as he said, laying each card upside down.

"This is how you found them? One, two, three, and in reverse?" He pointed to each card as he spoke.

"Exactly."

Tash bent over the cards, his hands on his hips, face set in concentration. "The Major Arcana are twenty-two cards that form the core of the Tarot. They tell a story of a spiritual journey. You found *The Fool* first. In reverse, or upside down, the fool can mean recklessness, or being taken advantage of. The second card you found is *The Magician* in reverse. This means trickery, illusions. They are also the first and second card of The Major Arcana."

I stood, squirming from foot to foot. "Someone is playing games with me. What are these? Clues this person knew I wouldn't understand? What is the third card?"

"*The High Priestess,* again in reverse and the third card in The Major Arcana. This means lack of center or repressed feelings."

I looked at Tash. I rarely let people get close to me, so how would anyone here know anything about me? Unless they were otherworldly beings themselves, like the witch standing next to me.

"Any idea where they came from?" Tash asked.

"Not one. At first, I thought they were random, left around town by locals. Somehow, I felt compelled to pick them up. It wasn't until the third card, which I found on my porch, that I realized they were meant for me."

Tash nodded, his hand cupping his chin. "Something else is definitely at work here. If I didn't know better, I would say there was another witch around. We'll have to be even more on our guard. Leave them here and I'll try out a spell later."

"Why not now?" I narrowed my eyes. This man had more than one mystery surrounding him.

"I have to prepare. We can do it now, if you like, but it will take some time. I promise not to touch them until you can watch, if that's a problem."

I picked up the cards and tucked them back where they came from. "I'll keep them with me until then."

"Suit yourself." He stepped back.

"So, first things first. We should start with Whitby—do some digging into his background, make sure he is who he says he is. I want to give him the benefit of the doubt. If he checks out, then we can figure out what to do from there," I reasoned.

"If he checks out, we need to educate him on the demon situation. The goal will have to be switched from the demons you say aren't the problem to the martolea. The first person to send them all back to their Hell dimension wins the wand."

"Agreed. I'm working with a local human. She's tech savvy and will be able to help with researching Whitby." I rose to leave. "I'll let you know what we find out."

"Uh, hold it." Tash held up a hand. "I thought we were doing this together. I'm not going to sit here and twiddle my thumbs. I'm coming with you." He walked over to the coat hook and grabbed his leather jacket.

I almost forgot I agreed we would work together. "Fine, hope you can keep up," I said as I moved past him and out the door. Trusting this witch was something I would have to do for the time being.

"Easily." He snorted. "Are you always this short with people?" We walked down the stairs side by side and out of the apartment building. Once on the street, he fell a couple of paces behind me, and I didn't bother to slow down for him to catch up.

"Actually, no. I'm known for being warm. My friend Bria says I have a calming presence," I answered over my shoulder. It was true. Bria often called me her yogi. She joked there was no one who could keep a cooler head under pressure.

"Ha. Right, calming. I'll just call you Selene the Sage."

He couldn't see me, but I rolled my eyes, pulling my mouth into an annoyed grimace. "Funny."

We walked the rest of the way in silence. I cautioned Tash to be on alert for martolea, but we didn't come across any as we marched single file like a couple of stormtroopers. Was there a method to their mayhem? I wondered if they struck at will or were led by some greater purpose.

"I hate to be that kid, but are we there yet?" Tash sounded a little winded as he jogged behind me. Keeping up with a vampire was not as easy as he'd thought.

We were getting close, the hill behind my rental looming in front of us. "Almost. It's on the other side of this rise. Getting tired?" I asked, derisively.

"I am mortal, you know. And almost forty." I wouldn't have taken him for being middle-aged. Tash had the smooth face and hard, fit body of a much younger man. I wondered if witches used their craft to prolong their health and beauty.

At the crest of the hill, I looked down and noticed smoke curling in billows from my chimney. Ileana must have started a fire. I forgot to ask her if she was comfortable before I left. I was glad to see she was helping herself, as I was clearly distracted.

Tash caught up with me. "Is that your place? Looks like you did a better job of finding lodging than I did. It's private, out of the way."

"For someone who has his own website, you must not know about vacation rentals."

"Actually, I do. You must have snatched the best one." He took off ahead of me. I wasn't the type to irritate people, and I typically kept to the background until the moment called for a more direct approach. I was under Tash's skin, that was evident. This would give me another advantage for the wand.

As we strode up to the front door, I called out, "I'm back, Ileana," so as not to startle her by throwing open the door. We found her exactly as I'd left her.

"Hey." Her dark, heavily lashed eyes peered over the edge of one of my ancient texts. "This stuff is crazy."

"Yes, it is," I agreed. "This is Tash. He's the other person I told you about, here to help with the demons."

"Hey," she said, again, her eyes moving back to the open book.

Tash waved a hand, although she wasn't looking at him.

"We need to switch course a little, Ileana. I have a feeling you will be a big help," I said to the top of her head.

She closed the book and set it down on the pile in front of her. "Okay, what is it? Assistant extraordinaire at your service."

"We need to look into the man who brought us here. Basically, we need to know if he is who he says he is."

She nodded. "Got it. What's his name and what do you know about him?" Ileana pulled her oversized bag toward her and dug around inside. She pulled out a pen and small pad of paper.

"His name is Joseph Whitby. He's a professor of history at Oxford, here in Romania on sabbatical. That's all I can tell you. I tried to look around myself before I came here and didn't find much." I didn't know a lot about our professor. The seriousness of knowing who you were working with couldn't have been more apparent. He could be anyone.

Ileana giggled. "It's enough. I'll find you everything you need to know. I assume this is an urgent situation?"

"It is. I have a laptop you can use. Hopefully, it still works. I recently dropped it." I retreated to the small bedroom and pulled my computer out of my satchel. I was more of a scour-through-books kind of gal, but the internet did come in handy from time to time. I suspected this would be one of those times.

A.D. BRAZEAU

CHAPTER EIGHT

Ileana pounded away on the keyboard, still sitting on the floor. Her fingers moved with speed and deftness, the clicking almost lulling me into a trance. I wanted to focus on what Ileana was doing, not having a conversation, but Tash had other ideas.

He sat behind me on the couch. I stood with my back to him, wishing he would call it a night. I had nothing more to say to him for the time being.

"How long do you think this will take?" he asked.

I huffed out an annoyed sigh, not bothering to turn around. "As long it needs too. Let Ileana concentrate on her task." This wasn't like me. If Tash and I hadn't been in direct competition for the wand, and if I didn't know he was a liar, I wouldn't have been treating him with such icy coolness.

"You could at least be hospitable." I heard Tash get to his feet. He opened and closed the door.

I shouldn't have, but I felt a little ashamed of myself. This witch was getting under my skin, as much as I was getting under his, not something I would usually allow. I turned around and followed him outside.

"Wait," I called to his retreating back. "I'm sorry. I'm

not here to make friends, but I didn't mean to act so crummy. I'm annoyed, tired of the run-around."

He turned back toward me, hands in his pockets. "It's not you. I'm not here to make friends either. This whole situation has me in a foul temper. I don't like being played with. I want the same as you, to complete this job and take the wand. Time is ticking away. This is a roadblock I don't need."

"Neither of us needs," I corrected. "Sit down. I don't have any drinks to offer, but we can at least enjoy the night air while Ileana does what she does."

Tash went to move around me, probably intending to sit. Instead, the toe of his boot caught on the lip of the concrete step and he pitched forward into me. I fell back into one of the hard plastic chairs, Tash's not unpleasant weight on top of me.

Rather than stand up immediately, he looked into my eyes. I swore I felt my breath catch as I gazed into his deep, brown eyes. This meant a lot because I didn't breathe. My lips parted, a sigh escaping, as he captured my mouth with his. I would have been shocked at myself if I wasn't enjoying the press of his lips against mine.

For a moment, it felt as if time froze. My brain screamed at me to stop, but my hands were on his chest, feeling their way around solid muscle. My body and mind were not in union.

Only when his tongue parted my lips did I snap out of my trance, pushing him back. That was a mistake. Never mind how long it had been since I'd been with a man, he was a witch and a liar.

"I'm sorry," he said, standing over me. "That was the epitome of inappropriate."

"It was and it wasn't. The kiss was nice, for a second. But we don't have the luxury of playing around. Sit down." I nodded my head toward the other chair. A wave of embarrassment fluttered through my core.

Tash let out a sigh. "Yeah."

Feeling some chitchat would help ease the tension and kill some time, I asked, "Where are you from? I detect a slight southern accent. My guess is Louisiana?"

"I'm from Baton Rouge, born and raised." Tash propped his ankle up on his knee, the manly way to cross legs. He reminded me of Alexandre in that position. "Ever been?"

I inclined my head as I thought about his question. "Once, but only to drive through on my way to New Orleans. I don't remember much about it."

"Ah, that's a shame. You missed out. Great people, sights, and food." His genuineness drew forth the first full smile on my face in days. "Best gumbo you've ever had at my dad's place, Carter's."

I pointed at my elongated canines. "Don't forget I can't eat. I've never had gumbo. It wasn't around in ancient times."

Tash laughed, shaking his head. "Again—missing out. My dad starts his gumbo at dawn, then lets it simmer all day to achieve peak perfection. Man, I could go for a bowl right now. There's nothing like a fall night in Baton Rouge, sitting on the patio of Carter's, jazz from the band inside, steaming gumbo in front of you. A Hurricane or two never hurts either."

"Sounds like heaven. I don't usually get to relax much, but I have indulged in a Hurricane."

"How long have you been?" He pointed toward my mouth.

"A long time. About 2,020 years."

Tash's smile disappeared, and his eyes went wide. "You're over 2000 years old? I thought you were kidding when you said ancient times. Wow, that's hard to wrap one's mind around. How does it feel to be that old? Or is that a stupid question?"

Now it was my turn to laugh. I could have liked this witch if he wasn't deceiving me. "It's not a stupid question. I feel as I did as a mortal, before I became ill, that is. Which is to say normal. Only there is no sickness, no pain from my body unless someone injures me."

He nodded slowly. Then shook his head hard once, as if to rid his mind of an unpleasant thought. "Weird, no offense."

I was about to say *none taken,* when he continued. "So, 2,020 years ago would have been right before the birth of Christ. What an amazing time. Which historical figures were alive then? Caesar?"

I bit my lip. This was going to be fun. "Julius Caesar died a few years before I was born. My half-brother knew him though."

"What?" Tash leaned forward so far in his chair I thought he might fall out.

"I'll put you out of your misery. My half-brother is Caesarion Ptolemy, the son of Caesar and Cleopatra."

"Your mom was Cleopatra? That means Marc Antony was your father."

I nodded as Tash's stare roamed all over me. "I can see it. I mean, I can see her, in you. Incredible," he whispered, taking it all in.

"Yes, it is pretty incredible." I thought about the Priestess card and its depiction of Isis. If Tash was the mastermind behind the cards, did he know of my connection to her or was it a crazy coincidence?

"Look, we have time to kill, and I need to hear this story." Tash scooted his chair, so we faced each other on the porch.

I sighed, looking up at the night sky. We did need to kill time. I didn't think it would do any harm for him to know. Besides, if he knew the Isis connection, he would know the rest. "I'll tell you my story if you tell me more of yours."

"Whenever you say," he agreed.

"All right, I'll start after what you probably already know; after mother's death, the boys and I were taken to Rome. We were young children at the time. Caesarion was gone, and it was rumored he was executed by Octavian, but I learned later he survived and was granted immortality by the same vampire who changed me. That's his story to tell. The boys disappeared, disappeared meaning they were also put to death. I was left alone, fearful for years I would be next. During this time, I did what I could to ingratiate myself with Octavian's sister.

"Over time, I proved myself to be a Roman in every sense of the word, my Egyptian side locked inside my heart for no one else to see. When I was of age, Octavian married me to his ally Juba the Second, the King of Mauretania. I became a queen in my own right. We ruled and lived together, happy enough, and had two children of our own. My son I named Ptolemy; he would also become king. I'm not sure what became of my daughter. I heard stories that she married and had children of her own, but any records concerning her are gone. Once I was changed, I stayed far away from them, fearful I would unwittingly hurt them.

"In my thirty-second year, I became ill with fever, desperately ill. As I lay near death, a young girl came to me. I was feverish and I believed the girl to be a figment of my imagination, a hallucination. She was named Layla, and she brought me into this life as I lay dying on cold marble. She had also changed my brother, Caesarion. Caesarion had left her and she thought I would make a suitable replacement for him.

"I remained with Layla in her cave for many years, until I, too, became restless. No longer content to remain locked away, I felt a need to be out in the world. Layla was mad. I left in the nick of time. Not long after I did, she set fire to herself and the handful of others who remained. In the time since, I have tried to dedicate myself to helping others. I truly believe this is my purpose."

Gaius Octavius Thurinus, also known as Augustus, would have despised the modern moniker of Octavian. I used it for exactly that reason.

There was more, a lot more, but I didn't feel this was the time, nor was Tash the person to get into it with. I was beginning to worry, though. At the time of Layla's madness, she was about the age Alexandre and I were now. Alexandre had gone briefly insane, only to come back to his senses. I wondered if my time was almost up. If it was, would I come around as he had?

"Wow, Selene. That's quite the story. That sounds like the short version but thank you for sharing. I imagine you have a lot to say about the intervening years, as well."

"I've moved in and out of civilization. There were times I was amongst it all, observing and taking part in equal measure. There were also times I was alone, wandering some wilderness or jungle, destroying the wayward beast. I've never felt firmly a part of anything, I guess. Always an outsider."

I hadn't meant to share quite so much. This was uncharacteristic of me. I wanted to trust Tash, to like him. There was too much about him I didn't know.

Tash didn't say anything for a beat. He looked at the mountains, his breath coming out in wisps in the cold, night air. "I bet you've been witness to some incredible events. You should write it all down."

My friend Bria had suggested I do just that; write our stories, maybe put them in a book, filed under fiction. I wasn't sure. There was a reason I told the story so succinctly. I didn't like to relive it. Relating my history in a cold, matter-of-fact way kept who I was in the past separate from who I was now.

As strange it must seem, after two millennia, I still missed my mother. I twisted her scarab ring around on my finger. I made the most of my circumstances, living my life the best I could, but Egypt and Cleopatra would always haunt me. Even after all this time, I could still see her face, still feel her strong arms lifting me in the air.

"You know, while you were ignoring me inside, I was thinking about the tarot cards you've found. I think we should go for a good old-fashioned reading."

I was sure my face conveyed the shock I felt. "As in a

psychic reading? Why don't you do the reading?" I searched Tash's face for any sign he was trying to pull something.

His eyes were steady on mine; there was no twitch, no flick of his gaze to the side. "I want to make sure the fall of the cards is not influenced by me in any way. Even if I try to keep the order completely random, my subconscious could still influence the order. You would be surprised how accurate any reading can be, if that's what you're thinking. If the person is skilled, they needn't be a witch. All we need to do is see how the cards fall for you. If the first three appear in the order you've received, then it stands to reason the others will tell us the rest of the tale. No need to wait for the next tarot cards to appear."

I bit my lip, unsure of how comfortable I was with this idea. "We don't have the time to spend on this. Do you think it would make a difference, knowing the rest of the cards?"

Tash shrugged. "They won't tell us exactly how all this will end, but they could help guide us, give us an advantage of a sort. Especially if the cards are meant as a warning."

In the end, I agreed. This was an interesting suggestion and one I wanted to see played out. Tash popped in the cabin to let Ileana know we would be back in about an hour. She wasn't pleased to be left alone again.

The glow from the computer screen illuminated her face as she narrowed her eyes at us. "Fine, but can you bring me some hot coffee?"

"Done." I winked at her and re-joined Tash outside.

As we walked toward the city, Tash pulled out his phone to locate a local tarot reader. In seconds, he had one. "Madame Alina; she has the highest rating in Brasov. You must love the modern age. What did we do before smartphones?"

The streets of downtown were bustling in the early evening. Aromatic food smells wafted from the restaurants. Car horns blared as a group of friends exiting a taxi stopped traffic in both directions.

Tash was walking a little closer than I would have liked, his hands shoved into the pockets of his leather jacket. "Cold," he mused. "I'm used to warm southern weather. I guess the temperature doesn't bother you much."

I wore thin black leggings under a blousy cotton tunic, a shawl thrown over my shoulders more to blend in then to keep myself warm. "Not much. I can feel heat and cold, although neither bothers me any."

"That must be nice. Can I ask you a question? Something that's occurred to me recently?"

I shrugged. "Ask me whatever you want."

"Do you have progeny? You know, those that you've made to be like you."

I gave a Bria-like snort. Tash had purposely avoided using the term *vampire*. He probably didn't want the many passersby to hear us. "No. I've never shared my gifts with anyone else. I only ever offered it to one person, and she declined."

It was true. I'd offered Bria the change not long after we met. The two of us had clicked right away, becoming family almost as soon as I arrived in Ireland. Bria had no desire to become immortal. I understood her reasoning. She wanted children and what she considered a normal life. It seemed she would now have all she ever wanted—with my brother.

"Why do you ask? Do you want the blood?" I watched Tash out of the corner of my eye.

He shook his head, vigorously. "No, thank you. Remember what I said about the merging of our kinds? I'd be hunted down quicker than you could say the word exterminate."

"Ridiculous. Witches are pretty backward if you ask me—no offense." I pursed my lips together to keep from laughing. I was quite sure I had offended and wasn't bothered one bit.

"Offense taken."

"My turn for a question. Do you belong to a coven?" Most witches worked in groups. I wondered why Tash was off by himself.

He rubbed a hand across his mouth. I had the feeling he was trying to decide how to answer. "There's a coven I belong to in Baton Rouge. They sent me here on my own for the wand. They didn't think it was as important as I do."

This was clearly a lie. I silently thanked Tash for reminding me he was not to be trusted. Any coven in their right mind would love to get their hands on an object as powerful as the Necromancy Wand. They either didn't know he was here or why.

Madame Alina was located across the street from the Black Church near Council Square. The gothic architecture was incredible. We stood across the street from the church for a moment to admire the exterior sculptures, arches, and tall windows.

I looked every which way, expecting to see another tarot waiting for me. This would be the perfect spot.

"Our psychic is over there." Tash pointed to the bottom floor of a row building.

Our destination was drab and unassuming. Only a flashing sign that read *Psihic* identified the business in any way. With some trepidation, I moved up the step and opened the door. A bell clanged above our heads.

Tash held the door as I entered the brightly lit room, empty of patrons. The space was decorated in very much the same manner as any waiting room in the world. Two plastic chairs sat along one wall next to a side table littered with decades-old magazines. Toward the back was a glass case which held various packs of tarot cards, incense, and candles, all covered in a fine layer of dust. On the walls were poorly framed prints of the Romanian landscape. Everything was sterile, bland.

The curtain behind the glass case looked like an entrance to a more interesting place. The thick fabric was a rusty red satin embroidered with golden thread. Tassels and little bells hung from the fringe.

Tash and I looked at each other. He shrugged.

After a moment, the curtain was parted by an old, arthritic hand.

"Come in." A deep voice, the English perfect, came from behind the curtain. All we could see was that one hand, shielded as she was. I sensed no malice, only an attempt at the dramatic.

I gazed back at Tash who held his arm out for me to go first. The inner room was nothing like the space out front. This area was dark, warm. An earthy incense burned on top of a scarf-lined bureau at the back, next to a closed door to yet another room. I imagined these old buildings were each a variable labyrinth of one small room after the next.

In the center of our current space was a low, round table, covered with yet another colorful scarf. The table sat on a deeply red Turkish rug. Pillows of blue, green, and gold surrounded the table.

"Please, sit," said the accented voice of the woman still standing in the shadows.

When she finally stepped toward us, it took everything in my power not to slide my eyes toward Tash. The woman, bent with age, was not my idea of a psychic. I was expecting a woman who wore bells at her ankles and a scarf around her head. This lady wore a black sweatshirt emblazoned with an appliqued kitten over acid-washed mom jeans. Her feet were bare.

I wondered if she would need help sitting but plopped herself down opposite us with the speed of a teenager. She pulled her legs into a cross-legged position. Her face was expressionless.

"I assume you are American, yes?"

"Yes," I said, not wanting to get into specifics. I knew better than to give away too much. She would have to read my cards without my help. "I'd like a reading, please."

I sat on a blue sequined pillow, then patted a green one next to me for Tash. This was his idea, so he better sit down. Never had I done something like this. I hoped it wouldn't take too long.

"Of course," she said. "What kind you like? Or shall I choose?"

I began to speak when Tash cut me off. "Could you do a Romany spread?"

Madame Alina rolled her eyes. When she looked at Tash, her lips were pulled down in a scowl. "Of course, I can. I am Romanian." Her sarcastic tone was not lost on either of us.

"Wonderful," Tash replied. "If you don't mind, we would just like to see the cards. We don't need an overall interpretation."

She ignored him and began to shuffle her cards as she looked at me. "A Romany spread will show you the past, present, and future. Remember, the future shown through the cards is dependent on the choices you are currently making. If you stay on your present course, it will end up as you see. If you choose a different path, other possible futures will emerge."

I smiled. Her words meant nothing to me. If we could change the outcome, why bother with cards at all? I knew my past. What I didn't need to see were history's events spread out on the table. I was beginning to feel irritated about the time we had taken to come here.

"We begin. Hold in your mind a question about the future," she said.

Madame Alina held the deck in her left hand, laying cards onto the table with her right. She laid them face down. When she finished, there were three rows of seven cards. I tried to take this seriously and thought of the immediate future here in Brasov. Would I figure out what was really going on?

"This row." She pointed to the row of cards closest to her. "Is your past."

I cringed, my shoulder visibly twitching. Tash laid his hand over my knee. The gesture was unexpected. My initial reaction was to brush it off as you would a bug. Instead, I allowed it to lay as it was. The warmth of his palm over the fabric of my leggings was soothing. I stirred a little as I felt something else. Was it a longing for more?

Madame Alina flipped the first card. "The Eight of Swords. The meaning of this card is imprisonment, entrapment."

A chill went down my spine. So, we were beginning with my kidnapping. Madame Alina watched me with a keen eye. I knew she was looking for reactions to play off. I maintained a placid visage.

She flipped the next card. "Justice reversed. This means dishonesty, unfairness. Seven of Wands—perseverance, maintaining control. King of Pentacles—hard work, responsibility. Queen of Cups—calm, comfort. Six of Cups—familiarity, happy memories." She paused before turning the final card of the top row, I assumed for dramatic effect. "The Death card. This is the end of the cycle and means change or metamorphosis."

Metamorphosis was right. I swallowed with difficulty. A lump formed in my throat. There on the table was my past, my mortal life from the moment Octavian took me until the night Layla changed me. It was unbelievable to see the cards laid out in this way. I cleared my throat, grateful for Tash's hand which hadn't left my leg.

"Go on, please."

Her hand reached for the first card of the second row. This row represented the present. She flipped the card. "The Fool in reverse."

My leg twitched. Surely, this was a coincidence.

Madame Alina continued. "This means you have been taken advantage of and can also mean inconsideration. The Magician in reverse—trickery, illusions. The High Priestess in reverse—lack of center, repressed feelings."

I noticed The High Priestess in Madame Alina's set of cards was also a depiction of Isis. This at least made me feel better. Isis must be a common character of this card. What didn't make me feel better was that these were the three cards I'd found thus far, exactly in order and in the same position. I began to fidget my fingers together under the table.

Madame Alina continued flipping in rapid fire. "The Tower—sudden upheaval, disaster. The Wheel of Fortune—no control, bad luck. The Lovers in reverse—one-sidedness, disharmony. The Chariot in reverse—lack of control, aggression. These cards represent your present." She paused again, letting her words sink in.

I was no expert, but this did not look good. Suddenly, I felt uncomfortable and brushed Tash's hand from my leg. There was not a single positive card in the lot.

"Would you like me to continue?" she asked, her keen black gaze penetrating mine.

I inclined my head. The need to escape the confining room was beginning to rise in the back of my neck, tension knotting the muscles of my shoulders.

"Your future." Madame Alina inhaled one long stream of breath. "The Empress—motherhood, nature. Nine of Swords—hopelessness, trauma. Seven of Pentacles—hard work, diligence. Nine of Wands in reverse—exhaustion, fatigue. Ten of Swords—failure, defeat. The Hanged Man—sacrifice, release. Death—change, metamorphosis." Madame Alina stopped. She looked down at the cards. All of us sat in silence for a good while.

"With the exception of a very few, I've never seen cards so bleak," she whispered.

I shifted positions on my pillow, drawing her attention back to me. She must have forgotten we were there.

Her eyes went wide. "Forgive me for saying that. How unprofessional of me," she sputtered. "Don't forget you can change the outcome of the future. The cards are not fixed. You alone are the master of your fate."

Tash pulled out his wallet, passing Madame Alina a wad of bills.

I rose to my feet then bolted out of the room. I had to fight the curtain, tassels flying, bells ringing, to escape. I felt as if I were suffocating in that space. The feeling was absurd as I had no breath. The tightness in my chest was there all the same.

"Selene." Tash caught up with me outside.

The cold air was bracing. It brought me back to myself like a slap across the face. "I'm fine," I lied. I was nowhere near fine. I didn't want Tash to see me so vulnerable.

"It's okay if you're not. That was the harshest reading I've ever witnessed."

I dropped my face into my hands, rocking on my feet. "Great."

"You may not see it now, but it gives you an advantage. Don't forget you can always choose a different course and change your fate. Madame Alina wasn't wrong."

"How are you supposed to choose a different path when you don't know what the paths are? I don't have a crystal ball. Do you?" I realized I was almost yelling. "Sorry. There's a reason why I've never had my fortune told. Let's get back. We've wasted too much time here."

We didn't speak all the way back home. By the time we reached my porch, I had formulated a few choice remarks. Before I could say anything else to Tash, Ileana burst out the door, stumbling onto the porch. "You guys check this out. Sit down, Selene."

I sat back in my chair. Ileana set the laptop she held in one hand on my lap.

"What am I looking at?" The screen didn't make any sense.

"No record of Joseph Whitby at Oxford. For good measure, I checked out all the top universities in England, and all the other Ivy Leagues, going back the last forty years, to be thorough. Nothing, nada, zilch."

"So, who is he then?" Tash asked the question we were all thinking. He and Ileana were bent over me, also looking at the screen. This threw a wrench into things.

Ileana straightened up, shaking her head. "No idea. There is nothing out there about Joseph Whitby except the two articles Selene already found. They look like plants to me. They were not published in any academic journals, only on an online forum, which is strange for an Oxford professor."

I looked up at Ileana. "Because he isn't one. This means we can't trust anything he says. He has some nefarious purpose for being here. We need to figure out what it is, while at the same time dealing with the martolea."

"The very demons he insisted are harmless. Which could tell us he has some sort of tie to them, right? What next, boss?" Ileana addressed herself to me. "Demon takedown?"

Ileana surprised me by her quick acceptance of the new world she had been thrust into. Again, I thought of my strong-willed Bria. I still wanted to learn more about Tash, but this seemed more pressing. He had given me a morsel about himself compared to what I shared. I couldn't shake the feeling there was more to this man. I hoped it was my general distrust of anything male, not the feeling he was hiding something that was nagging at me.

I closed the laptop, setting it on the ground. "Demon takedown."

A.D. BRAZEAU

CHAPTER NINE

Ileana needed a weapon. Since she refused to be left behind, I selected a large, lethally sharp hunting knife. The knife came with its own leather sheath which I attached to a belt and handed to her. "Keep in mind, this can hurt you as much as it can hurt a demon. Be cautious with it. Hold the grip tightly in your hand and don't hesitate. Hesitation can be fatal."

I would have liked longer to train her on the dagger, but there was no time. I felt better knowing she had something with which to defend herself besides her chest kicks. The three of us set out, Ileana and I with weapons in hand.

Although not as experienced a fighter as Bria, I had confidence Ileana could handle herself. She was a grown woman and I couldn't force her to stay back.

Tash was a different story. He wouldn't need the types of mundane hardware I carried. His protections were of a more supernatural nature.

Before we took to the mountains, we were going back to his apartment to collect some magical items. I still didn't fully trust him, but a short-term alliance would work well for everyone. I wouldn't let him too far out of my sight. I was sure Tash wanted the wand for some nefarious reason, as I'd thought before. Perhaps he even meant to sell it for personal gain, explaining why he was here alone. An object of such quality would bring an enormous price on the black market.

Tash and I walked side by side, Ileana a few steps behind. I wanted clarification on what he was bringing along. "Tell me what we're grabbing, again?"

"I need my athame and some herbs. An athame is a sort of ritual dagger. I use it to cast spells," he explained.

I hadn't ever seen a witch cast a spell with my own eyes. I was intrigued to watch, hopeful his magic would help us wipe out the pesky martolea in one fell swoop.

Tash's apartment still smelled of whatever brew he had previously been working on. "What is that odor, anyway?" I asked as we walked inside.

"I was working on a typical locator spell to find Whitby's demons."

This may or may not have been true. Inside the living room of Tash's rental, he pulled a battered, black metal box from underneath the couch cushion. The metal was scratched, rusty. I would have recognized it right away for a magical object. It pulsed with whatever it contained inside.

Tash set the box on the table, angling it away from Ileana and me so we couldn't see all the contents inside. I tried to crane my neck in a way which didn't seem obvious. I caught a glimpse of a patinaed brass bell, a writing quill with an ancient-looking crow's feather, and the curled edges of a black leather book. Nothing too special there.

Tash raised a compartment, pulling forth an object wrapped in cheesecloth. The lid of the box was swiftly closed. He shoved the box back under the tattered cushion and then went to the kitchen.

There were herbs hanging from the old, worn cabinets. Using regular shears, Tash snipped off pieces of several of these, a few I recognized. There was wolfsbane, wormwood, and thyme. The thyme was fresh, sitting in a bowl. Tash pulled out three sprigs, said a few words I didn't understand,

and then tucked one of the sprigs in his back pocket.

He held out the other two toward me and Ileana. "Here, stick this in a pocket, both of you. Don't lose it. It isn't much, but it will offer you some protection from evil."

I took the thyme, handing one to Ileana, and placed the sprig in the back pocket of my leggings as Tash had done. I didn't think whatever Tash was hiding would compel him to curse an eighteen-year-old. The fresh scent lingered on my fingertips. I watched Ileana to make sure she followed suit. I was glad she would have the extra help.

She held the herb in her hand. "What good will this do?" She took a whiff, scrunching up her nose.

"Just put it in your pocket. Trust me, it's better than nothing," Tash said. I may not have fully trusted him, but I did know a little about herbs and thyme was used in protection spells.

"It's okay, Ileana." I gestured to her pants pocket and she pushed it inside. I felt a small amount of relief from the tension gathering in my chest.

"Now, we fight. Is everyone ready?" I was eager to get to it. Ileana tapped her hunting knife and nodded. She looked a little nervous. Perhaps this would cure her of wanting in on the action. I knew I would feel better to have her back behind the computer screen.

Tash was stuffing his herbs into plastic baggies. "Almost." He took the baggies, slipping them into the pockets of his leather jacket. The plastic baggies made me think of school lunches, not witchy spells, and I laughed out loud.

"What's so funny?" Tash eyed me over his shoulder.

"I would have expected magical herbs to be placed in velvet pouches, not sandwich bags."

Tash's mouth twitched up at the corners. "Yeah, well, they're not magical until I make them magical. Plus, these bags are much more practical, and they seal." He held up one of the bags, flipping it in the air to make his point.

Finally, we were ready. I had my katana on my back and

my dagger strapped to my thigh. The only weapon Tash wielded was his athame, still wrapped in its cloth, which he put inside a pocket with the herbs.

As we walked down the stairs, I had an idea. "We should pop over and see what Whitby is up to. I want to make sure he's out of the way for tonight."

"You don't think your sword is a little conspicuous?" Tash asked.

He had a point, but I wasn't about to leave it behind. "Do you have a couple of towels?"

Tash went into the bathroom, coming back out a few seconds later with two dingy white towels. I slipped off my katana and wrapped the sword in the terry cloth. It wasn't ideal, but the late hour meant there would be few people out. I felt relatively safe I could keep the blade concealed enough until we were back out of town.

Tash's rental was only a few blocks from Whitby, and we were there in no time. It was late, past midnight, so there was no one about as I had hoped. This was not a town that kept late hours.

We stood in the darkness of an alley, across the street from Whitby's. The curtain of the front window was drawn. Ileana nudged my arm. "You can see a shadow moving around inside."

She was right. The light of the living room was on, and a figure, about the size of our faux-Oxford professor, was walking around. There didn't seem to be anyone else with him. I concentrated with my preternatural ears. There was no sound coming from the apartment except from the pacing.

"It looks like he's in for the night. Let's go. We'll be back to deal with him."

We made our way out of town and into the mountains in relative silence. I tossed Tash's towels on a pile at the edge of the forest. If all went well, we could retrieve them later. The surrounding trees shaded the moonlight, making it hard for Ileana to see. She had a hand on the back of my sweater as we walked. I was working out the puzzle of who Whitby really was when Ileana gasped.

I turned, keeping Ileana behind me as a twig snapped to my right. A giant creature stepped out from behind a tree. He was so tall, I had to take a step back to take all of him in. As Tash moved next to me, he pulled a bag out of his jacket.

"Wait," I said, holding out an arm in front of Tash.

The creature had not moved to attack. The varkolak was standing on hind legs, the fur on his body thick, matted with leaves and other debris from the forest. He blinked his eyes, standing his ground but not saying a word. I wasn't sure if he could. As with the strzyga, I sensed no malice. This was not the feral beast I met in Spain all those years ago. He blinked deep, brown eyes at us.

I took a tentative step forward, my hands up in front of me. "Hello. Can you speak?" If my heart could beat, it would have been racing.

"I can." His voice was raspy and thin, not as deep as I'd expected. "My name is Teodor. Why are you here, strigoi?"

"My name is Selene. The martolea are attacking and threatening innocent people. They're wreaking havoc on the town below."

The varkolak blinked again. "Those creatures are the foulest of the foul. They will do the bidding of any demon who snaps their fingers." This sounded like promising information. "The martolea were like us for a long time. They kept to themselves, feeding on wildlife, and they left the villagers alone. Then, one day, everything changed. They went back to the old ways. First, they only attacked those who came into the forest, then they were stealing and attacking humans from the city. They did not come to this on their own. Like us, they are a pack animal, they must be led."

"So, who is leading them?" I took another step forward.

He shook his head. "None of us know. All we know is there is something evil lurking, something new, new to us anyway." He started to back away.

"Wait, please wait. We could use your help. How many are you?" If the varkolak would help us vanquish the martolea, we would have this problem wrapped up in a bow in no time.

He stopped, appearing to consider me for a moment. There was a sadness in his eyes. "There are only three of us left."

"Three? Do you mean three in Romania?"

"I mean three in existence. My pack decided long ago that we would end our reign of terror on humankind, we would create no more like us. We were human once and we remember. This is no way to exist." He gestured to himself. I understood his meaning. The varkolakas were not as legend made them. They could not transform from wolf to human. These creatures were stuck in their forms, eternally werewolves. If they remembered what it was like to be human, I couldn't imagine how that must feel.

"I understand." I paused, weighing what to say. "You can assist us in ending the reign of terror the martolea are now involved in. Will you help us?"

"We will help you, strigoi." A female voice came from the trees. Two figures, slightly smaller than Teodor, emerged from behind him. "Those disgusting shapeshifters are depleting our food supply. Not only do they hunt humans once again, they continue to eat the animals we survive on. Their cave is on this side of the mountain about a mile in that direction." She pointed behind her.

A practical-thinking woman. I smiled. I did wish they would stop calling me *strigoi*, which brought images of Nosferatu to mind. "Thank you." I turned to check on Ileana. My two companions remained silent during this exchange.

Ileana's mouth was wide open. She did nothing to conceal her shock at seeing a werewolf in the flesh. "Ileana, are you, all right? You can head back if you want."

She closed her mouth with a snap and brought her

attention back to me. "Are you sure they won't eat me?" she whispered.

I heard a soft laugh from one of the females behind me. "They won't eat you. I promise."

Ileana wiped a hand across her brow, tucking loose strands of her thick, dark hair back into her headscarf. She took a deep, steadying breath. "Okay, I can do this."

I gave her a pat on the arm. I looked over at Tash, who nodded. This was new to both, but Tash was trying to affect an attitude of nonchalance, like he had conversations with werewolves every day. With that, the three of us followed the three varkolakas deeper into the woods.

A.D. BRAZEAU

CHAPTER TEN

The forest was as pleasant as always. The scent of pine was heady in the air. The silence was telling, though. Not a sound could be heard. In a forest at night, you could expect to hear nocturnal animals and insects. The quiet must have something to do with the martolea. I wondered how much of the wildlife they had wiped out. This made me even keener to destroy them.

We were moving at a quick pace. Tash and Ileana breathed hard behind me. I thought I was a fast walker, but the weres had me beat. I jogged up next to Teodor. "How many martolea are we dealing with?"

"At least twelve, maybe more. They roam in groups of two to four, so it's hard to know, exactly. Until recently, I wasn't paying them any mind." He strode past trees, his huge paws crunching leaves and snapping twigs heedless of the noise, his arms swinging at his sides. I imagined a human out for a walk catching a glimpse of one these beings as they walked through the trees. Would the human think they'd spied Bigfoot?

Twelve demons were a lot, no matter the species. I was grateful for the assistance the werewolves would provide. I knew I could handle a few on my own. Tash's ability had yet to be seen, and I didn't have a lot of confidence in Ileana, try as I might. Fighting a demon was not like fighting anything else. She had shown bravado in the street, but this was another equation. Take the unpredictability of a wild animal, mixed with supernatural strength and magical powers, and you had a demon.

There was a fine mist hugging the trees above our heads, which created an atmosphere of cold claustrophobia. I walked with the varkolakas, Ileana behind us, and Tash in the rear. Teodor looked over at me. "We are almost there. Prepare yourself."

I was ready. Ready to move through this obstacle and confront Whitby. The longer I sat with thoughts of the man, the more unsettled I became. He had something to hide, something big. The sooner we found out his secret, the better.

The cave loomed in the distance. The terrain became rockier. Ileana and Tash began to have some difficulty making their way over the rocks. It was quiet, not a sound to be heard.

I turned to help Ileana over a large grouping of boulders, when out of nowhere, I was hit in the back with the force of a freight train. I toppled over onto her, her back hitting the ground, hard.

The silence I noted earlier was broken by snarling, yelling, and snapping teeth. With a huff, I pushed myself off Ileana. "Are you okay?"

She grunted, feeling the back of her head with her hand. "I think so. Go."

I didn't need her to tell me twice. Twisting my body, I stood, staring down the martolea. It was wildly snapping its jaws, saliva dripping from its broken teeth. Its breath went in and out in huge puffs that stank like rotting flesh. The feral glow in its eyes focused on me alone. I wanted to look around, to see what the others were up against, but there wasn't the time.

Bending my knees and pushing off the ground, I

launched myself at the beast. I remembered the hole in my shoulder, so I kept my body low, tackling him around the lower part of his chest. I wrapped my arms around him, my fingers digging into his side as I pushed.

I slammed him onto his back, my knee pinning down his lower body. I moved one arm up and wrapped my fingers around his jaw, pushing as I did so to expose his neck. With my other arm, I whipped out the dagger strapped to my thigh. The beast yelped as I thrust the knife through its neck, severing its spinal cord.

There was no time to revel in my victory. I jumped to my feet, scanning the area. Ileana was standing behind me with her knife drawn. I was relieved to see her remaining where she was. She was in over her head and she knew it. Best she remained out of the way.

The three varkolakas were dealing with a group of demons about thirty feet from me. They were doing well— no need to rush to their aid. Tash was crouched down inside a circle he had drawn in the dirt.

He held his athame in one hand and was crushing one of his dried herbs in the other. As I watched he sliced into the palm holding the herbs, mixing them with the blood. He said something I couldn't make out, then let the blood and herb mixture fall at his feet.

Smoke began to fill the circle around him. With the dagger still in his hand, he flung out his arms toward a group of five martolea charging from the mouth of the cave. The smoke hit the three leading the pack and they dropped to the ground, unmoving. I was amazed and appreciative. This witch was a badass.

The two remaining shapeshifters broke off, one heading for Tash and one for me. I closed the distance, meeting mine head-on. I went to make the same move which had won me victory a moment before. I wasn't as lucky this time. This martolea lowered his head as he ran, making him a more difficult target.

I tried to jump out of the way but was a fraction too late.

He hit me in the knees, causing them to buckle. I fell to the side, the katana on my back clanging against the stones. I sucked in a breath as the demon sank its teeth into my thigh. I bucked my back, kicking my leg in the air, but the beast wouldn't let go.

I positioned my dagger to sink it into the creature's brain when the martolea readjusted its grip on my leg, sending a new wave of pain spasming through my body. It was so intense I dropped my knife. I beat my fists on the top of the beast's head, but it was no good. I felt the teeth hit my femur and started to become fearful I may lose my leg. It would reattach, but that would take days we didn't have. I reached desperately toward my dagger, muscle and sinew snapping.

I heard a grunt and felt the sweet sensation of the martolea's grip relax on my thigh. Ileana stood over the beast, her hands still around the hilt of her hunting knife which she had plunged into the shapeshifter's back. It wasn't quite dead, so I grabbed my dagger and plunged it into the brain of my attacker.

I fell back on the rocky ground. "Thank you, Ileana. You saved me from losing my leg."

She clamped her hand over her mouth, her face green with sickness. "It's so bad," she squeaked through her fingers.

"I'll live. I appreciate the help. You're a hell of a fighter. But for now, I want you to stay right here, understand?"

She nodded weakly, sinking back against a boulder. Ileana unwrapped her headscarf and threw it to me. "Wrap this around your wound."

I did as she asked, although there wasn't much need. As bad as it was, the wound would heal regardless of what I did. A yell from Tash brought me back to reality.

I spun on my good leg to see him bloody as well. With a gimpy run, I took off toward him. From the looks of it, Tash had taken a bite, almost as bad as mine to his arm. The martolea he was facing off with backed up to position itself for another attack.

My stomach twisted. I tasted bile in the back of my throat. Terror swept through me and I realized the terror was fear that Tash would die. Before I could reach Tash, the beast jumped toward him. Tash said something over his athame, then threw it at the heart of the beast. The enchanted dagger hit the demon true and it fell with a thud, dead.

Relief flooded through me. I collapsed onto my knees, feeling a little off from the loss of so much blood. "Where are the varkolakas?" I asked Tash, who was jogging toward me, heedless to his own injuries.

"Eating." His arm was oozing a steady amount of blood.

"Great," was all I could manage.

Tash dropped down on his knees in front of me, reaching out, likely unsure where to touch me. "That looks really bad."

"It is, but it will be fine enough by tomorrow. Maybe. Give me your arm." I reached out a hand. At least I could heal him instantly.

He pulled his arm away. "No, thanks. It'll be okay."

I rolled my eyes. "In order to become a vampire, you have to be drained and then drink my blood. A little blood in your wound will only heal you, nothing more." I continued to hold out my hand. "Don't be stubborn. We all need to be at full strength. Let me help you."

He hesitated, then let out a sigh. "Fine, but if I become a vampire, I'm never forgiving you. Besides, it looks like you need all your blood right now."

"I'm over two thousand years old. Believe me, I'll survive." I took his arm then smeared some blood from my leg over Tash's wound. The skin began to knit itself back together.

He sucked in his breath. "Wow, that feels weird and good." Tash wiped off his arm, moving it around to see all sides. There was still a deep red mark from the martolea's teeth, but the wound was closed. "Thanks."

The varkolakas joined us, blood and sinew dripping

from their mouths and all down the front of their chests. I tried not to notice. Tash had to look away. He must have seen enough blood and guts.

"We can't thank you all enough for helping. You've no idea the trouble you saved us," I said.

Teodor licked his lips. "It is done now, strigoi. We will retreat to our home. Good luck to you." Together, the varkolakas dropped to all fours, taking off deeper into the forest in a single file line.

"Not real wordy, are they?" Tash put a hand under my elbow, helping me to my feet.

"Who needs a conversation when they can fight like that? They saved us a lot of time and blood loss."

We walked over to where Ileana still leaned against her boulder. I dragged my leg behind me, hobbling the best I could. She looked less green. "I think maybe you were right. I'll leave the demon hunting to you two and I'll help from behind the scenes."

"We all have our strengths," said Tash, clapping her on the back like an army buddy. "Now what? We go check in on Whitby?"

"I think that's a good idea. I need to go home and change first. Since you can see the bone protruding from my leg, I'm thinking a bandage would be in order this time. Don't want to make people sick from the sight of me."

After a resounding victory, the three of us made our way back out of the mountains.

CHAPTER ELEVEN

Whitby was a liar. This we already knew, but what was the man hiding? Tash and I walked with Ileana back to my cabin after the battle with the martolea. Walked being a relative term as I mostly shuffled, dragging my leg behind me. Ileana needed rest, and I was too weak to protect her should the situation at Whitby's go south.

There was still the problem with Tash, as well. He had fought alongside us, diligently. Add this to the fact that he gave us a protection charm, kissed me, and kept touching me. I didn't trust him yet, but how could I deny the attraction? A big part of me hoped I was wrong about him and his involvement.

We went inside the cabin. My leg needed a little TLC before Tash and I took off again. As gross as it was, I pushed the bone back into place. Then, I tore long strips of an old sheet I found in the closet and bound my wound tightly.

"Text me as soon as you know what's up." Exhaustion was etched across Ileana's youthful face, her words coming out in a croak. The night in the forest had done a number on her.

"I will," I promised. "Please sleep. You need it."

She closed the door on us. I waited to hear the sliding of the deadbolt before joining Tash. The sun would rise in about an hour, so I didn't have a lot of time to dally.

We didn't have much of a plan, since we had no idea what was going on. We would confront Whitby with the evidence of his lies and demand to know the truth of what we were doing here, and how the martolea were involved.

The pain in my leg was intense, but even as I limped down the dim street, I could feel the muscles, ligaments, and skin working itself back together.

I decided to wait to feed until after we spoke to Whitby, to save time. It would have been helpful to have another vampire donate some blood for the cause, but there were none but myself. I had half a mind to mesmerize the witch and take a few swallows but refrained.

"Do you think Whitby could be dangerous?" Tash broke through the solitude with a question I had also considered.

I thought about his query as we walked side by side. "I think it's a good idea to have our guard up. He could be anyone or anything."

"He looks so harmless, though. A little old man in a tweed jacket." Tash said this like he thought it was funny. I'd known others who seemed as harmless at first glance, only to be surprised later.

"If there's one thing I've learned after this long, it's that appearances can be deceiving. If he's trying to trick us, dressing in the guise of a nerdy professor is a pretty good way to go about it."

Tash held on to my arm, pulling me to a stop. "Well, we know all about that, don't we? I owe you an apology, Selene. I was quick to judge you, and I want you to know that I trust you."

His words took me off guard. Tash's hand lingered on my arm, and it felt good. Since he brought it up, I needed some answers. "Did you seek out the wand? I called Whitby after I saw you that first night hunting the weres. He said you came to him looking for it. I don't want to believe him, but I honestly don't know what to believe anymore. I'm tired and I'm in pain."

Tash closed his eyes, his hand still on my arm. After a moment of silence, he looked into my eyes again. "Selene, Whitby is telling the truth. I did seek him out for the wand. I need it for something, something important. I can't tell you what it is, but please trust if I could tell you, I would. I'm sorry. I'm so sorry I can't tell you more. I don't want any harm to come to you or Ileana."

The anguish in his eyes was real. He was hiding something, as I'd suspected all along. How deep was his secret? How dangerous? I wanted so badly to trust him. It was clear I couldn't. Still, I needed him on my side.

"How did you know he had it?"

"There's a sort of signature given off by magical objects. I imagine it's like how you feel around demons and witches. You can sense them."

Okay, so he needed the wand. This need didn't necessarily have to be nefarious. There could have been all kinds of reasons for wanting the wand. "You don't owe me anything, Tash. If anyone should apologize, it's me. I was awful to you in the beginning."

"Selene, I…" Tash broke off his sentence and looked down at the street.

Something in his voice made my stomach do a flip-flop. I thought he was about to confess his feelings for me, so I took charge. I wasn't exactly ready for that. "Let's get through tonight and get the wand, which I'm keeping. Then we can see what happens."

Tash looked up into my eyes, his brows knit together, and his mouth turned downward. "Yeah," he said. Tash released my arm as we turned toward Whitby's.

After a few moments of silent walking, Tash asked, "How's the leg? You had me scared for a minute there."

I thought he must be uncomfortable with silence, the need to speak too much for him. Whereas I sought out silence, even with other people around. Tash seemed to need the banter. "Better and better every minute. It will be a couple of days, but by the night after tomorrow, all should be well."

"I must admit the whole healing thing is pretty cool. If there's anything I'm jealous of, that's it. But, living for eternity, I'm not so sure of." Tash walked with long strides. He planted each foot with surety.

"Eternity isn't for everyone. It can get to you if you aren't careful."

Tash turned his head toward me. "How so?"

I thought of the years, how many there had been. My past seemed like an endless tunnel of time. "Life can be lonely, immortal or not. It helps to either have companions or a solid purpose. I've had companions here and there, but my purpose has always been clear; to help others, to fight evil."

He looked to the other side of the street. I wondered why he did so. Did he feel guilty about something?

I thought of my husband, a man I hadn't thought of in a very long time. He was a king, and it was a different era. Although he was good to me, he did keep an occasional mistress. I always knew when he had a secret woman because he could never hold my gaze. Instead, he would look away, like a child who was caught in the middle of misbehaving.

"You had children, right? Your son became king, but you don't know what happened to your daughter?" Tash startled me with these questions. After so long, I often thought of my past as something that happened to someone else, like my life belonged on the screen and not in my head. To think too much on my children was too painful. It was easier to not think about them at all.

"That's right. It hurts to remember them." I struggled with the memories, wishing I could use my preternatural speed to get to Whitby's rather than having to walk and talk with Tash.

He sighed, looking back toward me. "I'm sorry. I can't

imagine how strange it must be to go on like that. No offense. Again."

I didn't answer, not because I was offended, but because he was right. My life, the lives of all immortals was strange. There was no way around the fact.

The attraction I felt for Tash would remain unrequited. It had to. Remove the fact he was hiding something. He didn't belong in my world and I didn't belong in his. Bria and Alexandre had gotten lucky. They were clearly meant for each other. Tash was only a handsome distraction.

When we were finally standing in front of Whitby's building, I could have breathed a sigh of relief. The time for child's games was over. I didn't have long before I needed to be back inside my own rental, so we would have to get to the bottom of this without delay. I needed a break from Tash. We were getting a little too close for comfort.

I went up the stairs first. Tash tried to hold my arm for support, but I moved it away. I didn't need him, or anyone else.

The door to Whitby's apartment was slightly ajar. I pushed it open all the way before stepping inside. All was quiet, and I didn't feel the presence of anyone else. This was wrong. Why would he leave with the door open?

I turned back to Tash and shook my head. We broke off, Tash to one side of the apartment and me to the other. We tossed the joint. I pulled out every kitchen drawer, rifling through mismatched silverware. The cabinets were next. All I found for my efforts were chipped dishes and a tin of Darjeeling tea. He must have taken his Earl Grey.

"Anything?" I called out to Tash.

He was pulling out couch cushions and tipping over furniture. "Nothing here. Bedroom."

Tash said what I was already thinking. We met at the doorway and he stepped back for me to enter first. I went to the closet, and Tash went to the chest of drawers. The closet was empty, not a single article of clothing had been hung up. "There's nothing here."

"The drawers are empty. He's deserted. Probably knew we were on to him."

I glanced around the room. "Maybe. Or maybe he doesn't need clothing or toiletries."

Tash opened the nightstand drawer. "What's this?"

I was behind him in a second, peering over his shoulder. "It's another tarot card—hand-drawn, like the others." Tash held up the card for me to see.

The tarot mystery was beginning to annoy me. "Which card?"

"The Tower."

"What does it mean?" I breathed into the side of his neck, trying to remember what the psychic had said. The card depicted what to my eyes looked like a lighthouse. Clouds and lightning bolts surrounded the tower on both sides.

"Disaster," Tash whispered. My blood ran cold.

"What do you have there?" Whitby's voice behind us made me jump into Tash.

We both whirled around, Tash still gripping the card in his hand. "You're a witch," Tash said, pointing The Tower at Whitby.

Whitby's voice had changed. I thought my ears must be deceiving me. The English accent was gone, and he sounded more feminine. "I'm not a witch, you useless imbecile. I'm much more than the two of you could ever dream to be with your small minds."

It was then I felt it, something I should have felt long ago. Whitby must have been skilled in masking what he was. The signature was suddenly obvious.

"You're a demon," I said.

Whitby looked at me through narrowed eyes, a half a smile on his face, which reminded me of a serpent. "Actually, I'm much more, Selene. I feared you would be the one to figure it out long before now. You, too, have been rather a disappointment."

But I hadn't figured anything out. I didn't want to let on

that I was completely ignorant, so I said, "Show us your true form."

Whitby cackled.

Tash grabbed my arm. "Are you sure that's a good idea? He could be anything," he hissed in my ear.

I wasn't sure but didn't think it mattered much. We were probably about to see Whitby in all his glory whether we asked for it or not.

As we watched, Whitby's skin began to slacken, hanging off him in folds. Tash's hand tightened its grip and I heard him suck in his breath.

Whitby's body became slimmer. Off went the tweed coat, slipping to the ground as the creature then began to grow taller. The sparse white hair became full and black, growing down to its waist. The features changed, morphing from those of an old man into a young, beautiful woman. The features were where her beauty ended. Her eyes were yellow, glowing with fire and malevolence. She smiled to reveal revolting teeth, pointed like little white triangles.

The clothing she was wearing, Whitby's white button-down shirt and tan slacks, fell away to reveal an outfit of red latex. The dominatrix effect was perfected by silver and black stilettos. She towered over us, and neither Tash nor I were short.

"Who are you?" I asked as I gazed up at this creature. She was beautiful in a frightening way.

"I am War."

I took half a step back, pushing into Tash, who stood partially behind me. She couldn't be War. If she was, that meant only one thing; she was one of the four horsemen of the apocalypse. I heard legends about them being female but never thought much about it.

"Yes, Selene. I see the thoughts working in your mind. I am a horseman. Slightly diminished without my sisters, but still a force to be reckoned with. You trapped me here when you closed Balor's portal, cutting me off from them. I used the guise of Whitby to call you here. You were supposed to help me take over this territory, creating my very own demon realm on Earth. Instead, you've slaughtered my only allies. You'll be sorry for that." She pulled her hand back, as if to throw some unseen magic at us.

"We won't stop, and you can keep your cards. I already know how the rest fall. Now that I know, I can change the outcome. Your game will blow up in your face."

A ferocious smile broke out across War's face, her sharp, white teeth gleaming. "You never really know someone, do you?"

Tash pushed me out of the way with such force I fell on the bed. He yelled words that sounded like a foreign language. A fireball erupted in his hand and before War could unleash her own power, he threw it at her. She fell back and disappeared.

"Did you just kill her?" I ran over to where she stood only moments ago. Was that all it took to end a horseman?

"No. The fire was meant to stun her, so we could run, but she vanished due to her own magic. What does this mean, Selene? Did she not have the wand?" Tash had a frantic look in his eyes. He gripped his bald head in both hands and walked in a circle around the room. He did need the wand, and badly.

"I'm pretty sure she has the wand, but she never intended to give it to us. Did you notice the burn mark on her hand as she tried to conjure her magic? Legend has it the wand leaves behind a burn in the shape of a figure eight; the symbol for eternity. You should know more about that than me. She's been using it or trying to. I'm guessing the wand can open a new portal. But, that's only a guess. We need to find out more about her, then end her, and we need more help." I moved closer to Tash. "Are you with me?"

"She must need this for whatever she's trying to pull. The Tower is an ominous card." He looked at the card, then back at me. "I'm with you."

CHAPTER TWELVE

The evening was cold as we left Whitby's apartment. Tash's breath curled in the night air. Our objective for the coming day and night was two-fold; research the horsemen and find the strzyga. I wasn't sure how willing they would be to help us, but we needed numbers, and more allies.

The varkolakas were gone, deeper into the forest. Their help had been a one-off. We couldn't count on them to assist us again.

I hoped the strzyga would stay out of War's way until we found them. I had sensed no malice in them and therefore worried she might destroy the seemingly gentle creatures. War wanted this area cleansed of any being who might oppose her.

It was a clever ruse to use me to do her bidding. She was smart. I felt some hope when I realized she couldn't do it on her own. In order to revel in her full strength, she needed her sisters. We had to do everything in our power to keep them from joining her in this realm.

Tash and I rushed back to my rental, my leg feeling better and better with time. The sky began to lighten as I ran. I was about to be sucked into blackness by the rising sun. While I slept, Tash and Ileana could work on researching our new foe, resting when they could.

We found Ileana curled up on the little couch, laptop on her chest, rising and falling with her breath. I handed the computer to Tash, then covered Ileana with a blanket.

"Guess I'll be taking the first shift." Tash sat at the dining table. "You don't happen to have coffee, do you? I could use some brain juice."

I rummaged through the cabinets. "Tea packets," I said, pulling them out to smell them. "They seem pretty fresh."

Tash was already pounding on the keyboard, pen and paper nearby. "Better than nothing. Just leave them on the counter, Selene, and go to bed. I don't want you hitting the floor."

He had a point; the sun was seconds away from shining its rays through the front window. "Okay. If there's an emergency, you can wake me, but it will difficult. And…you'll want to stand back."

"Got it," he said, not looking up.

"Before I head to bed, I have an idea. It only just occurred to me. I'm not sure I can do it on my own."

Tash grimaced, rising from his seat. He walked over to the box of tea, pulling one out and dropping it into a waiting mug. "What's that?"

I leaned against the door frame. The realization hit me that I was about to share even more of myself with this man I knew so little about, and who admitted he was hiding something. "I'd like to call on Nephthys, the Egyptian goddess of death. I'm not even sure we could raise her, but if we could, and she would help me, she could be a tremendous blow to our enemy." The idea to use any of the old Egyptian gods had never occurred to me before. Perhaps it was being faced with my brother and all the memories of our past that put the thought in my head now.

Tash stared at me for a long minute. "Sorry, what? You want to call forth a goddess of death while we're dealing with one of the four horsemen of the apocalypse?"

"Yes, exactly." I knew how it sounded, but I had my

reasons. They seemed reasonable to me at the moment.

"No offense, Selene, but have you lost your mind? I know you're Egyptian and all, but she could annihilate us. We have enough problems."

I smiled. Tash leaned back against the kitchen counter. "What do I not know?"

"She won't hurt us. Nephthys is sort of an Auntie. I'm a demigod."

Tash blinked, his brow wrinkling in thought. I wanted to continue torturing him, but the sun was steadily rising. "I'm the daughter of Isis and Osiris as much as I am Antony and Cleopatra. I can explain more later. Will you look up a spell while I sleep?"

Tash looked up at the ceiling in one long eye roll. "If you say so."

Smiling, I shut the door on the light and dove under the covers. Here I was about to black out with a witch I didn't fully trust on the other side of a flimsy piece of wood. I had very clearly lost my mind.

At sunset, I stumbled out of bed. I could have used a bath to clean my leg, but there were other pressing matters at hand. I stripped off my ruined pants and surveyed my wound. It looked better, but the bone was still protruding a bit.

My eyes squeezed shut as I pressed it further back into place. I tore up the good pant leg and wound it around the bone, hopeful that would keep it from ripping through another pair of pants. I chose the loosest pair of palazzos I had brought, not exactly good for fighting in, but the silky fabric felt wonderful against my sore appendage.

The scent of coffee and food greeted me as I walked into the kitchenette.

"I'm glad to see you two bought provisions," I said to Tash and Ileana, sitting side by side on the couch, bent over the laptop's screen. I noticed they were in fresh clothes, Tash in his usual black t-shirt and jeans, Ileana in jeans and a silky green tunic with matching headscarf.

Ileana grasped a steaming mug in one hand and was moving the cursor with the other. "Well, we can't live on blood, can we? We've also gone home to clean up. Tash was in desperate need of a hot shower. The quarters being close, and all." Ileana scrunched up her nose.

Tash nudged her with his shoulder. "You didn't smell very good, either." They laughed together, and I felt a twinge of something in my stomach.

"That's good. I take it we haven't had any demony issues while I slept. Did you find anything out?"

Ileana looked up; eyes wide. "Oh, we've found some stuff. You're going to want to sit down."

The coffee smelled good, so I poured a cup. It was no substitute for blood, which I was beginning to need quite desperately, but the hot liquid was soothing enough. I plopped onto the matching couch, across from two people I had grown to like.

I knew a little about the four horsemen, most people did. I was curious to find out what more they learned. My mind began to race with the possibilities, all bad.

Tash passed Ileana the notebook. She took it, flipping to the beginning. "So, War is the second horseman and she rode a red horse. They are depicted as men in the Bible, but since we know War is female, I will use the feminine pronoun. The first is Conquest, who rides a white horse. Number three, on her black horse, is Famine, and the fourth is Death, riding a horse that translates as pale. War's specialty is, get this, mass slaughter. There are several interpretations of what the horsemen represent, from the decline and fall of Rome, to the apocalypse." She paused to take a sip of her coffee.

I thought how odd it was the horsemen were thought to be responsible for the fall of Rome, when I was half-Roman. If only the reason were so simple.

"Tash and I believe, as far as how this will affect us, the horsemen must mean apocalyptic catastrophe. We doubt

Rome will fall, again. Clearly, War is here to cause some trouble. The fact that she's alone bodes well for us. If all four were together, we'd have no chance. As it is, she likely has the strength of a very powerful demon."

This was interesting but didn't tell me what I really needed to know. We needed solutions to our very imminent disaster, not biblical interpretations. "How do we kill her? Or can we?"

Tash set the laptop on the table, stretching out his legs. "That's the question we can't find the answer to. We've searched online and through your interesting collection of books." He indicated the pile of texts alongside the couch. "Granted you know more about your tomes than we do, so maybe you could look at those. It would make sense to send her back to where she came from, but apparently you sealed the portal we need to do that. So, Ileana and I are clueless."

"Speak for yourself." Ileana closed the laptop, leaning over to set it on the crate.

I sank back into the cushions. This was going to be complicated. I couldn't unseal the portal in Wexford. If I did, Balor would find his way back, and everything we'd gone through to vanquish him would have been for nothing. I didn't think Alexandre would like me to undo everything he did. He went to great lengths to seal Balor in the Hell dimension.

"It doesn't make sense for her to be here. If the portal she needs to re-enter her realm is the one I sealed in Ireland, what on earth is she doing here in Romania?" I chewed on my lip as I thought. She came here specifically for the wand. What does she want it for? Perhaps her sisters were meant to join her here. Closing that portal was absolutely the right move. It seemed there would have been more monsters than Balor running around. I rubbed at my hair. "We need to come up with a solution. Even if it sounds crazy, let's get some ideas on paper."

Ileana was the first to speak. "Well, we kill her. Why can't we do that?"

"Death would be ideal, and it's on the table. It isn't always so easy to kill something so powerful. Usually, with god-like beings, it's easier to trap them back in their own dimension. We could locate or open another portal. The problem would be moving War to a new site." I chewed the inside of my lip. "Wait...something we thought of last night. War may have been attempting to open her own portal with the wand. If it's even possible, we grab the wand, open the portal, and send her back. The trick will be to incapacitate her. Then we have to figure out how to..."

"I could bind her," Tash interrupted.

"Bind her? You mean magically?" I asked.

"Exactly. I'm familiar with how magical objects work. We both are. I'm sure between the two of us, we can figure out how to open the portal, if that was where you were going."

I mulled this over. It wasn't a bad idea, probably the best one we had. "It's the only solution that makes sense. We'll have to seal the opening after. Sealing a portal is not as easy as it sounds. To do so typically requires a large sacrifice of some kind, something as serious as a life. My brother gave up his immortality to seal the last one."

Tash leaned forward, his face hard and serious. "We'll have to figure that part out when we get to it, I guess."

Our eyes met. Something unreadable lurked beneath the surface. Warning signs went off in my head. I chose to ignore them. "How long could you bind her for?"

"Ideally, an hour or two. If I really had to push myself, I could hold her for a few days at most. It would take a lot of energy to hold her that long. I'd have to stay up round the clock."

"If you think you can do it, it's probably the best idea we have. Hopefully, you won't have to hold her for too long."

"I can work on getting everything I'll need ready while you enlist the strzyga. If you think we still need them. As for your other request; I found a spell to raise Nephthys. It's more a generic spirit-raising spell, but with a few modifications, I can tailor it for your Egyptian goddess of death. We can only do it once, so you better be sure."

"Why only once?" Ileana asked the question I was already thinking.

Tash took a breath, shaking his head. "Energy. I only have so much to give at any one time. Expend too much and I'm out of commission until I recharge. Binding War seems the most important current use of my energy."

I was determined we should do this. "I understand, Tash. She'll help us, I know it. And, if this works and she agrees, Nephthys could end it all without the need for a binding spell and portal. This means we'll need even less energy from you."

Ileana pulled at her scarf. "Do you really think that's a good idea, Selene?"

"It will work. Nephthys was known as a kind and useful goddess. She will help us." I sounded more convinced than I was. At the least, she would deny our plea for help. If she agreed, however, the time spent on the endeavor would be worth it.

Tash handed me a folded piece of notebook paper. This was the spell.

"Let's do it." I fidgeted with the paper, an unfamiliar quaking rippling through my belly. "I feel like this is the time. We can use her now. If she says yes, we can leave the strzyga out of this. If she says no, then we've lost nothing." I glanced up at Tash. "Other than your energy, that is."

Tash shook his head. "We don't know what will happen, Selene. It's best to wait until we feel we have no other option. Use her as a backup."

"That would be the worst time to call her forth. To raise a goddess of death at a moment of crisis, unsure what she will do? No, I say we do it now. If she can or will help, she'll come forth of her own volition when it counts, no need to raise her again."

Tash and Ileana looked at each other. "She's not going to budge on this," Tash said to her. "Fine, Selene. We need to clear the room as much as possible."

I jumped off the little couch, fear and excitement rolling through me in waves.

Tash stacked the dining table and chairs in the bedroom. I pushed the two small couches into the recess of the kitchenette. The coffee table-crate was shoved against a wall. This left us with a decently sized space in the living area for our spell.

Tash advised Ileana to stand back. She sat on one of the couches in the kitchen, pressing her body as far back into the cushion as it would go, hugging her knees to her chest.

"Selene, lie here—on your back. Spread your arms and legs like the points of a star." Tash indicated the worn rug under our feet.

I did as he said, feeling awkward spread eagle on the rug. Tash placed an assortment of odd-sized candles fished from the kitchen drawers above my head and next to each hand and foot. I felt like a virgin about to be sacrificed in a pagan ritual.

"No one speak or move." Tash flipped off the lights, leaving us in total darkness. I heard Ileana suck in her breath.

A match flared above me, the acrid scent of sulfur filling the air. Tash touched the flame to the wick of each candle. They sparked to life with a crackle and pop. The room glowed in a warm, soft light. Shadows danced across the walls with the flick of each flame.

A warm hand on my shoulder made me jump. "Are you sure about this?"

"Do it," I whispered.

"I'll need some of your blood, okay?" Tash moved alongside me. He gently raised my hand in his, his stare intense. I nodded once.

Tash looked terrifying in the light of the candles, not at all like himself. His features were contorted, as if he held a flashlight in front of his face to tell a scary story at the campfire. I flinched as a blade ran along the flesh of my palm.

"Sorry," he breathed.

Blood poured forth from the wound, collecting itself in a white bowl Tash held underneath the flow. I continued to lose blood when what I needed to do desperately was feed.

"That's enough," he said.

I licked the wound, healing it with my own form of magic, then laid my arm back as it was.

Tash moved behind my head, out of sight. "Close your eyes and concentrate on my words."

As my lids descended, Tash began to chant in low tones. His incantations never made any sense to me. The longer I listened, the more I began to realize he was repeating the same sentence over and over.

For a moment, I was confused, unsure whether I was hearing him correctly. The more I concentrated, the more I understood. Then, a feeling of calm washed over me. I lay still, in a trance as the words seemed to penetrate the very air around us.

Within minutes, something started to happen. The space was alive with electricity. The hairs on my body stood on end and my skin crawled with the sensation of thousands of ants. I kept my eyes closed. I knew the magic was working. Trepidation wormed itself inside my chest. I smothered it. Fear had no place in what I did.

There was shouting—confusion. Was that Tash yelling at me? I tried to open my eyes, to sit up from the ground. Something had gone wrong. Wind whooshed around me, battering my eardrums so badly, I thought they may burst.

Then, all was still. The air changed from charged and alive to breezy and humid. My eyes fluttered open. I stared up at a familiar mural; a Roman couple sat in their colorful garden, a child at their feet playing the lyre. The figures were clad in flowing tunics, their round faces beaming with happiness.

Nearby gulls squawked, barely audible over the crashing of waves against what I knew was a rocky shore. The oleander in a vase near my bed gave off a sickly floral odor.

I sat up from the bed with a start. It couldn't be. How real it looked. There on the blanket chest was my collection of seashells, silver and white against the brown of the leather.

As a child, Octavia would take me to the beach, my hand held tightly in her own while we explored. Those shells represented countless hours strolling with the woman who became my surrogate mother. On a pillar next to the terrace door sat a bust of Octavian, a gift from the man himself.

Nausea rolled through me. I leaned over the bed, my stomach heaving into the chamber pot. I was human. I had to be; vampires don't throw up. Sick, shaking violently, I wiped the spittle from my chin.

A woman's laughter, loud and bitter, filled the room. Behind the gauzy bed curtain stepped a figure. She was dressed as an Egyptian queen in a gold beaded net dress dotted with fiery red and orange stones. Her ankles and wrists were wrapped with strips of dark-blue silk, like the wrappings of the dead. On her head, she wore a headdress in the shape of a house and basket.

"Nephthys," I said. "Why have you brought me back here? I don't understand what's happening. My friends and I need your help."

She looked at me. Her eyes were hard, her mouth a straight line. "Help? Why would I assist a daughter of Isis?" Her tone of voice was contemptuous, spiteful. She stood over me, an ugly sneer smeared across her face.

"Why wouldn't you? You were a good and helpful goddess. I don't understand. I thought you could ferry War back to her dimension, as you once did for mortals who crossed over."

She huffed. "Isis and Osiris left us alone in the dark, alone to wither, to die. Being more powerful, they went on to a new place, the rest of us suffering in blackness. You've called me forth, back into the light. For this, I thank you, but now I will punish you for the sins of your parents. You can't cheat death, daughter of the moon, no one can."

Nephthys disappeared with a peal of thunder.

"Wait," I called. She was gone. The goddess pulled me here, back in time. How would I get to Brasov?

"Are you still in bed, my lady?" Sarah entered the room, her feet touching the marble floor so gently they made no sound. I was startled to see this woman from my past, a face I had not seen in 2,000 years. She was the same as I saw her last, a small figure wrapped in white, her mousy, brown hair tied up behind her by a strip of linen.

Thinking back to my time in Rome, I tried to get a handle on when exactly I was. "Yes, I'm ill."

Sarah's practiced face remained passive. She placed a cloth over the chamber pot before taking it out. She would be back to help me dress. I needed to come up with a plan.

Breathing deeply, I moved my feet to the ground. I remained perched on the side of the bed until Sarah returned with a tray of wine and grapes. She placed this next to me on the bed.

"Your bath is ready, my lady. Do you feel well enough?"

"No, I need some time alone, Sarah. I'll let you know if I need anything else."

She inclined her head, leaving me by myself.

My options seemed few. An appeal of some sort would have to be made to Nephthys. I supposed I could play along for a short time, until I had my bearings. What could this forgotten goddess want? If I figured out her desire, how would I deliver it?

The nausea was passing. I attributed the sickness with the abruptness of being pulled back in time. The plump, red grapes looked delicious. It had been so long since I'd eaten solid food.

I plucked a fat fruit from its stem and popped it in my mouth. The sweet juice exploded across my tongue. It was heaven. Within the span of a couple of minutes, I devoured the lot. The dark, fruity wine was also partaken of.

My limbs were heavy, as if not fully awaken from a long

sleep. I massaged my arms as I walked languidly to the terrace. The sight took my breath away. What a juxtaposition to the modern world I currently inhabited. The deep-blue sea was dotted with small fishing boats, rolling on the gentle tide.

Shirtless men, their backs hard and brown from long hours in the sun, threw handwoven nets into the water then pulled them in with varying degrees of success, dumping their catch at their feet.

I gripped the stone wall, throwing back my head to allow the sun access to every inch of my face. The brightness felt heavenly. The sharp rays hurt my eyes. This mattered little as the warmth touched and heated my skin.

As I held onto the wall, a scraping sound drew my attention to my hand. I hadn't noticed it before. A small band of gold inlaid with emeralds lay on the index finger of my right hand. This ring was a gift from King Juba before our marriage. The present had been made about a week before the ceremony. Another kind of nausea rolled through me.

The desire to relive my past was nonexistent. Those years were played out, over. I had to get out of here, now. The situation in Brasov was dire, and wasting time languishing here was not an option. I dashed back inside, my feet slipping on the smooth stone. The bath would have to wait.

I dressed in a soft blue tunic, draped over one shoulder. Around my waist, I clasped a thin, gold chain link belt. My fingers shook as I buckled simple brown sandals. I always loved this style of dress. It was free, comfortable, and feminine. Even in the modern day, I was drawn to flowy, natural fabrics in soft, muted colors. This was all I desired to hold on to.

From my modest jewelry collection, I selected a brooch of gold laurel leaves. This would come in handy shortly. Privacy would be needed to call forth Nephthys. I couldn't risk Sarah or anyone else walking in on me.

There was a small sanctuary on the edge of the garden that overlooked the sea. Octavia often went there to be alone when the demands of her household became too much for her. If my timing was correct, she would be elsewhere, busy with preparations for my wedding. My eyes and ears were open to anyone who might waylay my mission as I left my bed chamber.

I walked down the cool corridor with the air of someone who knew what they were about. As I walked, I ran my hand from one column to the next, marveling at the splendid home I occupied so very long ago.

Everything was pristine, every slab of marble, every statue and tapestry was of the finest in the land. The familiarity of this place struck me again. Even after 2,000 years, I knew this villa like the back of my hand. Every corridor, every room, was as known to me as my own face.

There wasn't time to truly reflect on how I felt here. Although familiar, the feelings welling up inside me were anything but homey. All I ever felt in Octavia's home was fear. The question of *When will they come for me?* always in my mind. For a time, I thought they were torturing me with the uncertainty.

Octavia cared for me, of this I was sure, but Octavian, I never trusted him for a second. I may have locked the past away, but I always remembered what he did to my mother, father, and brothers.

When my marriage was announced, I realized I was an asset to Octavian, a political pawn. To survive, I played my part well. King Juba was a lucky choice. He was good to me, allowing me freedom and the ability to rule at his side as an equal. I could have easily ended up in the hands of a despot.

The green of the garden peeked out ahead of me. With a quicker pace, I continued down the hall until I reached the stairs. A look around confirmed I was alone. I jumped down the steps two at a time, nearing twisting my ankle in the process. It could break for all I cared. Once I hit the gravel path, I broke into a run.

The little circular, marble building was topped by a copper dome. The metal glinted in the sunlight like a beacon. I rushed in, grateful to find the room empty. There were sumptuous cushions strewn across the floor. Flowers floated in bowls set around the outer walls. This would have been a lovely place to relax.

I kicked the cushions out of my way, sending one into a bowl, water sloshing onto the floor. Sinking down on my knees, I took a deep breath. I had no idea if this would work. The brooch was torn off my dress and the pin sank into the flesh of my palm. I bit my lip to keep from yelping. I pressed my hands together, squeezing the blood onto the marble floor. The red stood out darkly against the gray and white swirls.

With my head bowed, I recited, to the best of my ability, the words Tash had spoken over me. Almost immediately, a strong wind swept through Octavia's sanctuary, sending pillows flying. The porcelain flower bowls hit the walls, shards exploding around me.

"What do you want now, Selene? Tired of mortality already?" Nephthys stood in front of me, her eyes narrowed, her arms folded tightly across her chest.

"Please, great Nephthys. I don't belong here. Send me back. I'm your kin, aren't I? Those people in Brasov, they need me."

She threw back her head, the same hateful laugh from earlier echoing around me. "I'll decide where you need to be."

"What can I do? What can I give you for my return?" I pleaded with her. Gods were not easily persuaded. Once angry, it was hard to dissuade them. I had to think of something.

Nephthys looked at me with such concentration, I thought she may be considering my request. Her head snapped from side to side. "What's happening?" she whispered.

I looked around. Nothing was different. Then I felt the

air around me change, become electric. Her attention returned to me. "He's trying to bring you back." She spit out the words, eyes burning like flames. "I'll teach you, Selene. Our lesson is far from over."

On her last word, my body began to whirl as if being sucked into a vortex. The force exerted on my person was extreme. When I thought I could take no more, everything stopped. Blackness. I remained still in the dark, terrified to find out where I could be.

As my eyes adjusted, I saw the candlelight flickering across the wood beams of the A-frame cabin. Relief washed through me.

"Selene, my God." Tash was bent over me, yelling in my face.

Ileana stood behind him, hands clasped over her mouth. Beads of sweat were running down Tash's face, his breathing ragged.

"I'm okay." Standing was difficult with wobbly limbs. Tash helped me to my feet, one arm around my shoulder. His touch felt so good. We stood for a moment until the shakiness passed.

"Where did you go?" Ileana asked. "One moment you were here, the next you disappeared."

Tash released me. "I figured she must have taken you, but I had no idea where. It took everything I had and a lot of improvising to pull you back."

I collapsed on the sofa, still tucked into the space of the kitchen. Tash looked like he'd been through the wringer. Aside from the sweating, he was shaking, and his eyes were drawn, making him appear as if he hadn't slept for days.

"Thank you. You didn't have to do that for me. It would have been so easy for you to leave me there."

An undistinguishable expression flickered in Tash's eyes. He bent down in front of me, reaching out a hand for my knee. "I would never leave you or anyone else to an unknown fate."

Warmth bloomed through me. I smiled. The sentiment

was real. Still, I moved my leg out of his reach. His gaze fell to the floor at my gesture. I wounded him, but there was the whole trust thing that wedged between us.

"Where did you go, Selene?" Ileana repeated her question, drawing my attention away from Tash. "We were frantic."

"Ancient Rome. About a week or so before my wedding. Thankfully, I didn't stay long. I've no desire to repeat the past."

Ileana stood with her eyes wide, her head shaking. "Rome? Whoa..." She swayed as if she might faint. Tash moved to her, guiding her onto the couch next to me. I realized Tash knew more about me than Ileana did. I would have to rectify that soon.

"Yeah, whoa. It was Nephthys and she was angry. So angry I can't believe this is over."

Tash raised his eyebrows. "I'm not going to say I told you so. Now what?"

"Now we carry on. If Nephthys comes back, I'll think of something." I didn't tell them of Nephthys's threat. Now wasn't the moment when we had so many other problems. It was time to get back to the mountains. Nephthys, I would deal with alone.

CHAPTER THIRTEEN

The crescent moon looked eerie, ominous to me; half-shrouded by heavy clouds. I took to the treetops, delicately leaping from branch to branch.

I hoped after my warning, the strzyga, being half-owl, would be hiding themselves up in the highest boughs. I had long been fascinated by these creatures and would have loved the opportunity to study them more. Perhaps one day, I could return to Romania to research and rest.

Legend had it the strzyga were females, born with two hearts, two souls, and two sets of teeth. These abominations were thrown out of the village to live life on their own. Often, the creatures would die early. Upon death, one soul would go on and the other would remain on Earth, preying on people for their blood in the form of an owl.

In reality, strzyga were fully formed beings. They were almost entirely owl-like, except for their long, crone arms and human-like hair. When they stopped preying on humans, I wasn't sure. It seemed the change in diet was brought about by a need for self-preservation.

The strzyga were strong, frightening creatures, but they were not terribly powerful. The only supernatural powers they possessed, that I knew of, were immortality and the ability to fly. This made them vulnerable to human retribution.

About halfway up the mountain, I sensed I wasn't alone. Crouching down in the top of a swaying oak tree, I scanned the area. Two strzyga were perched not far from me, a few trees over, their bodies almost hidden by the fragrant boughs. I wondered if they traveled in pairs, or if these were the two creatures I already encountered.

I made my way silently down the tree trunk until we were parallel, then made my presence known so I wouldn't startle them by purposely snapping a small branch. Enormous, liquid eyes moved in my direction. They stood, ready to take flight.

"Please don't be alarmed. I would like to speak with you, if I can." I tried to read them for any sign of friendliness, but their collective gaze remained blank. "May I come over?"

The strzyga looked toward each other. Without exchanging any words, they looked back at me and nodded in sync. Trying to be as non-threatening as possible, I eased my way toward them until I was sitting on a branch opposite my new owl friends.

"Thank you. I expect it's much nicer for you to have the martolea gone, isn't it?" I thought a reminder of how my colleagues and I cleared the mountain of the foul beasts would be a good place to start.

The strzyga farthest from me startled me by speaking. "Once wildlife becomes more plentiful again, we will be less hungry."

I didn't think this was much of a thank you, but for a second, I was lulled by the creature's voice. There was a hooting quality to the back of her throat, the tones soft and muted.

"It won't take long, I'm sure." I paused. These human-sized birds wouldn't help us. I didn't know what I was thinking. They couldn't even help themselves. "I was going to ask you for something, but I see now I was mistaken. I'll leave you."

I moved to go back the way I came. As I did so, the other strzyga held out a long, spindly arm. "Wait. What were you going to ask?"

I re-settled myself. "One of the four horsemen is trapped in this dimension. I'm not sure if you're familiar, but she's a destructive entity. She wants to take over this territory as her own and open a demon portal. Her name is War, so you can imagine what the area will be like if she can take hold. The good thing is, she's alone for now. Her followers, the martolea, are all gone, and her sisters are in another dimension. I was going to ask if you would help us contain her so my friend can work a binding spell."

The strzyga who had spoken smoothed her chest feathers then looked to her companion. They again gazed at each other without speaking for several seconds. Were they telepathic?

She looked back at me. "My name is Tindrah, this is Cida."

"It's a pleasure to meet you both. I'm Selene. Have we met before, here in the forest?"

Tindrah shook her head. "No, strigoi, we have not met. My sister and I will help you. As for the others, only they can speak for themselves. We will go to them now. Where can we meet?"

I told her we would meet at the clearing in front of the martolea's former residence in one hour. They agreed and took off into the air. For such large creatures, they flew with lightness and grace.

I texted Ileana and Tash with the plan, asking Tash to meet us if he could. Once we had a strategy in place with the strzyga, we would alert Ileana and get started.

Waiting by the cave took a lot of patience I didn't have. I wondered where War was keeping herself and what her plans were. She must have a scheme of some kind. I didn't think losing her furry friends was too much of a blow for her, being one of the most frightening biblical terrors there was.

Tash answered my text, saying he was almost finished preparing what he would need for the spell and would meet me. True to his word, he was twenty minutes early.

I heard the crunch of his boots on the hillside before I saw him. "Not trying to be stealthy, I see." I didn't know why I was feeling playful, but I was. I hated to admit just how much I liked him.

He smirked. "What's the point? I figure if I'm alone and in the sights of one of the horsemen, I'm done for anyway." Tash carried a large, black duffle bag slung across his back.

Feeling strangely overcome with emotion, I turned around. I knew he was joking, but the thought of losing Tash caused a surprising pain in my chest.

Tash came up behind me. "I'm sorry, Selene. Did I upset you? I was only kidding."

I turned around to face him, confused. I wished I didn't find him so attractive. How much easier this would all be if I didn't. "Why can't you tell me what you're hiding? I know there's something."

Tash looked down at his feet, fists clenched by his sides. "All I can say is there is a person more important than me who I would die to help."

My chest constricted. I felt like I had been kicked in the stomach. "A woman," I said, my voice small.

Tash looked at me, his eyebrows pushed together. "Not in the way you think," he breathed.

The warmth of his eyes shone wildly in the moonlight. His breath was coming faster, and I knew he felt what I did. I couldn't trust him, not entirely, but I wanted him. Before I knew what I was doing, I had his back pushed roughly against a pine tree.

This was not the ideal location for lovemaking, but I didn't care. I could sense other beings and we were squarely alone. Still, this would have to be fast.

Tash grasped my upper arms with strong hands, bringing me even closer. My lips hovered over his for a split second before he closed the distance, capturing my mouth with his. My head tilted to the side as our mouths parted, hungry for each other. This was so out of character for me, it was shocking. Somehow, this thought made it hotter.

I melted into him, hands roaming his muscular chest. His body was so hard, so masculine, he made me weak in the knees.

Tash slid down the trunk of the tree, taking me with him. I straddled his waist as we continued to kiss. His hand pushed its way under my shirt and began kneading my breast, gently. I moaned into his mouth as he pulled down the lace cup and rolled my nipple between his thumb and forefinger.

I pushed my hand down between our bodies to unbutton his pants. His erection, large and ready, was waiting for me. I stood to peel off my pants, then straddled him again, this time with naked thighs.

Tash brought his hands around my buttocks and guided me onto him. I had to bite my lip to keep myself from crying out as he penetrated me.

"Oh, Selene," he breathed as I began to slowly ride. Never would I have thought myself the kind of person who would jump a man outside for anyone to see. Tash did things to me that didn't make sense.

Vampires felt sensations more acutely than humans, and this was overdue. It wasn't long before I was crying out in a great spasm. Tash gripped my backside with more force, bringing me down harder and harder until he, too, was crying out in the night. He hugged me to him, burying his face in my neck.

A sound out of human hearing alerted me to potential witnesses. "Someone's coming." I gently released Tash and stood to retrieve my clothes.

"Yeah, we just did," he said as he buttoned his pants. "Sorry, that was crass."

I laughed. "But funny."

Tash threw me my pants. "We should probably talk about all this."

"Now's not the time." I pulled up my pants, suddenly unable to meet his gaze.

"Where are your new friends? Is that who you heard?"

I looked up at the sky. "Yes, they're on their way. We don't have all night, let's go."

A whooshing sound filled the air. Where a moment ago there had been nothing but stars and the moon, there were now at least a dozen owl people, wings extended, gliding on the breeze toward us.

"They're kind of beautiful in a freaky way," said Tash next to me.

We stood back to allow the creatures space to land. They alighted before us, one after the next. I was glad to have anything other than Tash to focus on.

I tried to pick out Tindrah and Cida, but it was pointless. Each strzyga looked identical. I was sure they must all have different markings, but I didn't have the time to figure it out.

One strzyga broke off from the others and waddled forward. "We are here. Tell us what you plan to do, strigoi."

"Tindrah?" I asked.

The strzyga blinked her enormous eyes and dipped her head.

I gestured toward Tash. I had to put what just happened out of my mind and focus on the task at hand. "This is really your show. What do you need?"

Tash surveyed everyone around him, seeming to mull over his idea. "I've prepared a powder." He pulled a vial from his pocket, handing it toward me. "When this preparation is blown into War's eyes, it should stun her, knocking her out for a minute or two. She must be still for the binding spell to hold her. While she's stunned, I'll go to work. I can't set up anywhere. It will take a bit to prepare everything I need."

"So, we'll have to lure her to you," I interrupted.

"Exactly. Do you think you can do it, Selene?"

I looked at the ground, gathering my thoughts. This was where the owl-creatures were going to help us. "We need to locate her first. Can you speak to each other telepathically?" I asked Tindrah.

She nodded. "Perfect. I need you all to fan out, searching Brasov and the mountainside. When your people have a location, they can alert you, Tindrah, who will be with me. You and I will go to War and snatch the wand. She needs it for something. It's important, so she'll come after us. We'll dash back here, where I will stun her, and Tash can perform his spell. Does that sound too convoluted?"

Tash chuckled. "A little, but we don't have all night to come up with a Napoleonic military strategy. Let's do it." He looked around, surveying the area. "This will be a good place to work. There is space to move and we are far enough removed from the city that any noise will be minimal."

"Okay. What about your people?" I looked at Tindrah.

She turned around, looking at all the faces in turn. When she moved back to face me, she said, "We are ready."

"Let's not waste any more time. Please, everyone, set out now."

With that, all the strzyga, except my new friend, took off into the night sky, each flying in a different direction.

I wondered how long it would take to find War. In the meantime, I could help Tash set up. "What can I help with?" I asked him, trying to avoid looking directly into his eyes.

He moved farther into the clearing and dropped his bag on the dirt. The duffle was unzipped to reveal all manner of magical objects. Tash held up a piece of white chalk. "Draw a large circle, using me as the center. You must remain outside of the circle at all times."

I took the chalk, doing as he asked. I wondered if he felt as awkward as I did. I still couldn't believe what we had done only moments ago. Butterflies took off in my stomach as I thought about doing it again.

As I crouch-walked around him, I watched what he pulled from his bag. There was his athame, which he placed near his knee as he knelt. There was a brass bell, a pestle and mortar, and several plastic baggies of various herbs. He set out the worn, leather book I had spied in his box of magical tricks, along with a bundle of something I assumed to be sage and a small broom I knew to be called a besom. A besom was used to sweep away negative energies. Boy, did we need that.

When I finished drawing my circle in the dirt, I tossed the chalk into Tash's waiting hand. He bowed his head, going to work with his instruments of magic.

As I watched, he took the same piece of chalk and drew a pentacle in front of him. Next, he took his baggies of herbs. From these, he grabbed a pinch here and a sprig there, throwing each ingredient into his mortar. When he had all the herbs he needed, he closed the bags, neatly placing them back inside the duffle. He was neat, meticulous.

Tash pulverized the contents of the mortar with the pestle and set it aside. He grabbed his athame and sat back on his heels in the dirt. "Now, the last ingredient we need is War."

CHAPTER FOURTEEN

Tindrah and I waited, Tash kneeling in the same position within the circle. She sat perched like a graceful lady on a boulder. I kicked at the dirt with impatience and not a little anxiety.

Tindrah cooed softly then fixed me in her calming gaze. "War has been found. She's in a cemetery, not far from here. Cida says she appears to be waving a long, strange wand around."

War had the Necromancy Wand and she was waving it around dead bodies. That couldn't be good. I held out my arm. "Lead the way. We better hurry, I imagine War is trying to raise the dead."

Tindrah took flight and I followed along on the ground, keeping her in sight. I rushed through trees, over boulders and streams, never taking my eyes off the sky. A little more than three miles from where we were standing moments ago, Tindrah pulled back to land next to me.

"We're close now," she said, standing closer to me than she ever had. "Cida and I will distract her while you take the wand. War is over that ridge." Tindrah pointed with one wing to the small slope of the mountainside in front of us.

This was it. I was about to face a horseman of the

apocalypse with two owl-women. The absurdity of the situation hit me in the face. "All right. Let's move quickly. And Tindrah, don't put yourselves in unnecessary danger. Flee if you must."

She nodded, and we split up to do our parts. Tindrah once again took to the air as I crept silently up the incline. Creeping was as natural to me as drinking blood, so I had no problem sneaking up to the edge of the cemetery without War seeing or hearing me.

The cemetery was one of the more interesting I had seen. Carved into the side of the mountain, not a single headstone stood straight up and down. Each one was off-kilter, tilting to one side or the other. The smell of decay didn't come from the graves, instead, it wafted from the mossy wet, overgrown grass that covered every mound.

I found a nice, tall headstone to hide behind, wonky though it was. War was in the center with her back to me, hands out, with one clutching the wand, like a conductor. As I watched, something was starting to happen.

The ground under my feet began to rumble, like quaking earth. This could only mean one thing; the dead were about to rise. She needed new minions and what would be better than undead soldiers? This would be the definition of bad.

Now was the time to act. I rose to my full height and ran at War with my full speed. Above me, the strzyga circled the graveyard. War, startled by the commotion, flinched back. Tindrah and Cida swooped down, clawing at her with their rear talons and then flew back up in the air, out of harm's way.

War looked up at the skies and cackled like a cartoon witch. "Do you think a few birds can stop me?" she yelled. She pulled the wand back, readying to aim it at one of my feathery friends.

"Not so fast, War!" I yelled as I barreled into her.

The force with which I hit her knocked the wand out of her hand. Tindrah dove down, wrapping one talon around the object, and once again took to the air.

Before War could unleash any unholy blasts in my direction, I sprang off her, bolting out of the cemetery and back down the hill. Looking up, I spotted Tindrah overhead. "Tindrah! Drop the wand to me!"

Tindrah released the wand right into my waiting hand. I stopped running, taking refuge behind a pine tree to make sure War was in pursuit. She was. Although fast, she wasn't as fast as I was. This was a blessing, as I could run ahead and taunt her enough to keep prodding her to continue.

War had powers of which I was unaware, and I had to be sure to stay far enough out of reach.

"Come on, War. You can run faster than that, can't you?" I yelled from the safety of my tree.

"Slow and steady wins the race, don't you know that by now, Selene?" Her voice was cool, calm. She didn't sound like someone in much of a hurry to recover her property. War wasn't scared of me one bit.

A tendril of fear began to wind its way down my spine. I shook it off. She wasn't as powerful on her own. We already knew this. War was a practiced deceiver and knew what she was doing. I took off at a dead sprint.

Shaking off my doubts, I continued. I only needed to get her near the circle, blow the dust which sat in my pocket in her face, and the rest was up to Tash. This was going to be easy.

A boom like that of a firework went off behind me. Continuing to run, I looked back. War was gone. I thought when she disappeared in the apartment she had run out the door with preternatural speed. Now I realized she could teleport. I cursed myself for being so stupid and stopped in my tracks.

As I did so, an unseen force wrenched my arm behind my back. "Let go of the wand or lose your arm, Selene. Do you have the time to rest while it reattaches?" War had me in a vise grip, the skin around my shoulder starting to separate. She was right, I didn't have the time for it to heal. I didn't have the time either way.

"All right!" I screeched. "Take it."

At the same time as her grip on my arm slackened, I heard the whooshing of wings. I spun around as Tindrah and Cida attacked War's face with their talons. War tried to beat them off the best she could but ended up falling backward. Black blood poured from open cuts on both her cheeks and from a deep slash down the center of one eye. She screamed.

"Go!" I yelled, but it was too late. War pulled back a hand, unleashing a fiery blast at Cida. The beautiful strzyga was dead before she hit the ground.

An ungodly moan escaped from Tindrah. I had to get her out of War's way. "There's no time. Fly, now!"

Tindrah moved out of the way as another blast burst forth from War's palm. She was safely in the sky and I was moving with all the speed I could muster, the wand clutched in my hand. I wouldn't be stopping to taunt War now. The only thing that mattered was getting her into the clearing and making sure she couldn't hurt anyone else.

Minutes later, and I was there. Tash was nowhere to be seen, but I could feel him. He was hiding nearby. War crashed through the branches of a tree along the perimeter, coming up right behind me. She wasn't playing any longer, either.

"I was hoping to spare you, Selene. I thought perhaps the two of us could work together. It's a shame, really. Think of all we could do. But those thoughts are long gone. You are a nuisance I must extinguish."

I wheeled around, dust in the palm of my hand. "Working with you would be the last thing I ever do." Holding up my hand, I blew a fine mist of the magical dust into War's face.

Her body froze, although her eyes continued to dart all around. "What did you do to me?" She could still speak, her voice twisted and hoarse.

"That would be my doing," said Tash, emerging from behind a boulder.

Tindrah alighted onto the ground next to the chalk circle, her eyes watery and sad. I wanted to go to her, but Tash and I had to get War inside the ring. Tash pushed War backward and she fell, stiff as a board onto the ground.

"Grab her ankles," Tash directed as he placed his hands under War's shoulders.

We walked her to the circle, Tash in the lead. Making sure my feet never crossed the chalk line, I leaned down, depositing my end of War right inside. I took a step back, joining Tindrah to observe the binding spell. I tentatively reached out, placing my hand on her feathery shoulder.

When Tash had War positioned alongside the pentacle, he said. "I'll need absolute silence."

Tash lit his bundle of sage, waving it over the body of War, then rang his bell three times. He sprinkled the herbs from the mortar in the center of the pentacle. When he picked up his athame, War spoke.

"You don't want to do this, Tash." Her voice was becoming weaker, more difficult to understand. "Don't you want to see Grace again?"

Tash's body tensed, and he moved forward, grasping War by her elbow. "What do you know about Grace?"

Who was Grace? I wanted to ask, but Tash asked for silence. I waited to see how this would play out. I was confident Tash was too smart to fall for any demon tricks. Or…was this the woman he had spoken of before?

"I'm the one who has her, of course."

My stomach turned. Something was happening here.

"No. A demon named Dru has her. You're lying, trying to weasel your way out of this." He twisted her elbow then sat back on his heels.

"I'm not lying. If I wasn't stunned, I could show you Dru's form. She has spiky green hair, small red horns, and yellow eyes, does she not?" War tried to turn her head toward Tash. Instead, her eyes rolled in his direction as far as they would go.

"It doesn't make sense." Tash shook his head. I wanted

him to look at me, meet my eyes, but his head remained down.

War hissed. "But, it does. I enlisted you and Selene to rid me of my enemies. I could have let the signature of the wand lay dormant. I know magic, too. Instead, I released it so you would come to me. The one witch with a true tie to the wand. Wasn't it your ancestor who died with the wand in her hand?"

I stood, creeping my way toward the pair in the circle. My palms were starting to sweat. A true phenomenon of fear for an immortal.

War slid her eyes toward me. "I was planning on seeing to it that you win, after Selene did most of the work. I do hate getting my hands dirty. In return, I would give you the wand, and you would hand it right back to me, in the form of Dru, of course. Call your daughter another insurance policy. I thought it was all rather brilliant. My enemies vanquished without having to raise so much as a finger. Then, gaining a powerful ally or two in the process. It hasn't worked out as I'd planned, but you can still have your daughter back. All you must do is let me go. I give you my word."

My hand flew up to my mouth. War had Tash's daughter? That was why he was here, and why my instincts told me there was more to him than he was letting on. She was the girl he would die for.

I continued to inch forward. "Tash, you can't trust the word of a demon. You know that. Bind her now, and I will help you get Grace back. My word you can trust."

Tash looked up at me, worry creasing his brow. "I'm so sorry, Selene." Tash clapped his hands together and a bright flash knocked Tindrah and me backward.

My head smacked against a stone. Rubbing the back of my skull, I leaped to my feet. Tash and War were gone, along with the wand.

CHAPTER FIFTEEN

"That low-life. I knew he was trouble." I was hopping mad, pacing back and forth in my tiny living room. I finished relaying to Ileana all that occurred on the mountainside.

Ileana's hand had been clamped over her mouth for five minutes. She was more shocked than I was. She stood on the far side of the couch, eyeing me and Tindrah in turn. Ileana wasn't comfortable with the strzyga sitting in the room.

"You can't really blame him for wanting to save his daughter, Selene. Can you?"

"I can blame him for not trusting me to help him. He manipulated me with his kiss, and his touches, and his..." I stopped. There wasn't any need to go into too much detail.

Tindrah sat, perched as well as she could, on the edge of a couch cushion. I doubted she was very comfortable indoors but had insisted on coming along after she and I walked back to Cida and buried her where she lay. Tindrah wept over the body of her sister, then wiped her tears and vowed to avenge her. I hoped she would get the chance.

Ileana dropped her hand from her face. "What are we going to do?"

I sighed, unsure where to begin. "The first thing I want to do is go by Tash's place and see if he left anything behind. Maybe we'll get lucky and find a clue as to where they're headed."

I felt for Tash in a way. If all War said about his daughter had been true, I couldn't really blame him for betraying us. On the other hand, dealing with demons was never a fair proposition. I was sure she wouldn't give him back his child, no matter what she said. War had lost too much ground. She needed every advantage she had. Tash was a big advantage.

Tash's apartment was dark from the street below. Ileana and I stood on the sidewalk, Tindrah on the roof's ledge above us. I opened my senses and ascertained the apartment was deserted.

I forced the locked door and went inside, Ileana peering over my shoulder. She crossed to the living room window, opening the pane for Tindrah to fly into the room. There wasn't much for her to do as her rounded body made it difficult for her to move in the space, but she wanted to be with us. Her presence was calming, and I was glad she chose to remain.

"What is all this? This stuff gives me the creeps." I turned my attention to Ileana, who was bending over the small kitchen table.

All manner of strange items littered the tabletop; dead spiders, a rusty nail, coffee grounds, thorns, burnt flower petals, drops of dried blood, and a sigil. The sigil would only be able to be interpreted by the witch, as it was a symbol of the desired outcome of a spell or curse.

"Don't touch anything. These are ingredients for a curse," I said, trying to make sense of all the pieces.

"Who was he cursing?" Ileana whispered, fear in her trembling voice.

I bent closer to the sigil, carefully looking over the symbol etched into a piece of wood. Something that looked like a fang was drawn into the center of the piece, surrounded by triangles, an hourglass, and another symbol I couldn't place.

"Me." I straightened, refusing to be upset over this. I should have known better; the blame could only be placed squarely on my shoulders.

Ileana gasped, reaching out to touch my arm. "Was he successful?"

I shrugged. "Of course, he was. Not only did he leave with War and the wand, he succeeded in making me trust him."

"We all trusted him, Selene. Don't beat yourself up." Ileana still held onto my arm with a light grip.

It was too late for that. I couldn't see a time when I wouldn't be beating myself up over this. "Let's see if we can find anything else."

Ileana and I tossed the place with zero grace. We left no stone unturned but didn't come up with anything we could use to find Tash or War. All the while, Tindrah sat silently on the coffee table, waiting patiently for us to finish.

I flipped a chair back over and sank into it. "Nothing. Where on earth do we even begin?" I was feeling defeated. Never had I been so close to giving up on a case.

Tindrah surprised me by speaking. "The only logical place seems to be where magic has already taken place."

Tindrah didn't offer anything else, but she had me thinking. War wasn't terribly powerful on her own. She now had Tash on her side, so perhaps she would abandon her scheme of raising skeletons and go straight for opening the portal. But where?

I tried to think of where anything magical had happened recently. I thought of the tarot cards and the locations of where I found them. Nothing especially magical had happened. I simply picked up the cards.

It was then I remembered what War had said as Mr. Whitby. He had found the wand in Bran Castle. It seemed an awfully specific place. Why not say he found it in the woods? Was Whitby lying or had War let something slip? "Thanks, Tindrah. I think you may have won the day. We're going to Bran Castle."

"We're going to Vlad's castle? In the dark?" Ileana did not sound happy.

"No. I'm going. The two of you have done enough. I want you to stay here. Keep an eye on the village."

Ileana crossed her arms, affecting the attitude of a disgruntled teenager. "No way. I'm going too. I may not have vampire strength, but I'm going to do my part. You shouldn't be alone."

"As am I." Tindrah's soft voice was an octave higher than normal. "Don't forget about Cida. She was my sister. I owe War a fight. The others are finished, but I will help you. I must."

I smiled at my new friends. "Well, there isn't much I can say, is there? We go as soon as the sun is down tomorrow. Tindrah will fly. Ileana, you will travel with me, on my back."

"On your back? Like a baby?"

"No, like an adult. I can carry more than you could imagine. By the time you get there using human means, too much time will have elapsed."

Ileana looked dubious but didn't say any more. Before leaving the apartment, I picked up the sigil, placing it in my pocket. I needed to know more about it.

Back at my place, we prepared to head to the castle the next night. Ileana didn't want to be alone, so she took a shower and changed into some of my waning supply of clothes. I insisted she try to eat something, but she said she couldn't.

Tindrah went out to feed on the wildlife, returning before dawn to settle down alongside my bed. I could have fed too but would be fine for a while longer. I prepared the best nest I could for Tindrah with blankets and towels. Ileana would try to sleep as well, although she still seemed spooked by the curse ingredients and our next expedition, so I figured she would be up all day.

When we were all settled inside, I barricaded the door and both windows. I didn't think this meager furniture would be able to stop War if she chose to send a blast at the house, but it made Ileana feel safer. I hoped Tash would at least care for Ileana's welfare, if not mine.

Before lying down, I laid out the weapons we would take. My katana and my thigh-strapped dagger were my go-to choices. Ileana would again carry the hunting knife, and a small Ruger handgun. I was not partial to guns, but Ileana knew how to handle them. She was known to hunt with her father from time to time, and I thought this would give her a way to defend herself while keeping her body at a safe distance.

As I lay in the squeaky bed, springs pressing into my back, I thought about the last couple of days. I had begun to feel hopeless when faced with ending Balor's reign of terror, but that didn't compare to the hopelessness that now bloomed inside.

We couldn't even be sure War was heading for the castle. Tash's betrayal was a dagger to the heart I would never confess to anyone. One thing comforted me; as an immortal, I was safe from any scrying magic should Tash attempt to watch me.

I didn't want to think of Tash. Nonetheless, his image filled my mind; chiseled face, strong shoulders, bright smile. What I didn't want to admit to myself was this feeling of despair had more to do with him than anything else. I liked him, a lot. I didn't want to, but there it was. At least he helped me prove to myself what I already knew and somehow forgot; help many, trust few.

My phone buzzed on the bedside table. I grumbled, limbs heavy as the sun was rising. The text was from Alexandre.

Selene, I need you. Millicent has gone missing.

A.D. BRAZEAU

CHAPTER SIXTEEN

My eyes flew open with the setting of the sun. I had blacked out before I could respond to my brother. Without further delay, I pressed his number.

"Tell me what's going on. I'm in a rush," I said when Alexandre answered.

"Annie, Thayer, and Jack are here. They arrived last night in a panic. Millicent was last seen walking beside the lake behind her chateau. That was two nights ago and there is no trace of her."

I could hear the fear in Alexandre's voice. I wondered how sick, pregnant Bria was dealing with all the otherworldly visitors. "All right, I'm close to finishing up here. I'll be with you tomorrow night." I hoped this was true.

When Alexandre said goodbye, I caught a hitch in his breathing. He was terrified. I had to remain focused on what was in front of me before I could help my brother.

It was time to travel to the portal and make War suffer. I stripped, changing my leggings for jeans, not something I wore often. My leg was now almost fully healed, so the fabric didn't cause me pain.

I was ready to head out. More drama awaited me after

this was settled. I longed for a break from it all.

I opened the door of my cramped bedroom, pulling a soft ivory sweater over my head as I walked. Neither Tindrah nor Ileana were anywhere to be seen. From the doorway, I could see a piece of paper lying on the kitchen table.

Ran home to grab a couple of other things.

The note was short and gave me no indication of when Ileana had left. Tindrah must have gone with her. I couldn't imagine why Ileana would leave when she was so nervous the night before. She knew I wanted to leave right away, so it made me a little anxious that she wasn't back yet.

Eyeing my duffle bag sitting next to the door, I decided to go to Ileana's apartment, hopefully intercepting them on their way back to me.

I snatched up my belongings, locked the front door behind me, and took off over the hill toward the city. My feet moved swiftly, but not so fast that I would look unnatural to any mortals who were out and about.

The night was cold, a bracing wind sending chills up my arms. I would be fine, but I would need to remind Ileana to dress appropriately. No doubt the interior of the castle would be freezing.

Being Friday night, there were a few more people out then I was used to seeing. I picked up the pace, eager to make sure Ileana was all right, and even more eager to get on the road. My katana was safely out of sight in the duffle, and the dagger around my thigh was hidden by the length of my sweater.

The corridor of Ileana's apartment building was deserted. A fluorescent bar light flickered above my head, making me feel a little uneasy. As lightly as I stepped, the floor still creaked under my weight.

My stomach dropped as I neared her door. It was ajar. Not only ajar, but the wood was cracked and split where someone had kicked it open. I dropped my bag and pulled the dagger from the strap around my thigh.

I stood in front of the half-open door and listened. There was nothing inside, not the breath of a human nor an electrical signature from a witch or a demon. Still, I was cautious. I remained standing where I was, my hand reaching out to push the door open the rest of the way.

The room was in shambles. I walked into the entryway and peered around what was once a nicely decorated room. Pink throw pillows lay haphazardly on the ground. Two white, modern dining chairs lay on their sides, one broken into pieces. Framed art prints were askew on the wall.

I strode down the short hallway and into Ileana's bedroom. This room looked mostly untouched. A bag, half-packed, lay on the pretty, floral bedspread, a few pieces of clothing on the floor.

My heart sank; War had Ileana, possibly Tindrah, as well. Why had she taken my friends and left me alone? Tash knew where to find me. It didn't make sense. She knew I was heading her way, and now I was heading her way with murder on my mind.

As I was contemplating how to secure Ileana's front door, my phone buzzed. It was Tash, and my stomach dropped again.

Meet us at the cave.

Fearing the worst, I closed Ileana's door the best I could, grabbed my bag, and took off into the night.

I kept to the treetops, hoping to observe my enemies before descending. As I neared, I left my bag in the top of a birch tree, removing my katana and strapping it on my back. Then, I made my way from tree to tree as lightly and soundlessly as possible. I hoped the height would keep me hidden from Tash in more ways than one.

It didn't take me long before I saw the clearing in front of the cave up ahead. I settled onto a branch and peered down below. Ileana was the first thing I saw, bound and gagged and lying on a flat stone. She appeared to be unconscious. Tash was kneeling close by, grinding away with his mortar and pestle, his other magical paraphilia in the dirt next to him. I didn't see War or Tindrah.

A soft rustling to my right drew my attention. I looked over to see the top half of Tindrah's head, her giant, round eyes barely visible over the bough of a tree branch. She blinked her eyes and nodded her head. I took this to mean she was with me. I returned her nod, took one more look around, and jumped to the ground like a panther.

Tash was startled, falling backward as he flinched. I ran toward him, kicking over his mortar, herbs pouring into the dirt.

"Wait, Selene," he whispered, looking around. He braced himself with one hand and held up the other, like that would stop me.

Leaving a witch with free hands was never a good idea. I moved behind him, pulling him up by his shoulders and wrenching both his arms behind his back. It would have been so easy to make them stumps. As it was, he did yelp in pain, which brought me some joy.

Tindrah touched down, trotting immediately over to Ileana, who was starting to come to. She moaned, moving her head from side to side. As Tindrah helped Ileana, I focused on Tash.

"Where is War?" I spoke into his ear, sure that War couldn't be far.

"She's close. She's bringing my daughter, which is why we have to move fast." He tried to free his arms, but I wasn't about to fall for any tricks.

"What do you mean *we*? You're with War, not us. Tell us what her plans are before I pull your arms off." I tightened my grip to put a little oomph into my threat.

Tash sucked in his breath. "Okay, you're pissed. I get it. Selene, we don't have time for this. War has my daughter. If I don't help her, or at least pretend to help her, she will kill my Grace. I'm all she has, Selene. My daughter needs me."

"Pretend? I saw the curse ingredients on your kitchen table, Tash, along with my sigil. I know what you are."

"You may know what I am, but you don't know everything. I was working a curse on War and a protection spell on you. I had your sigil in my shirt pocket, and it must have fallen out. I didn't know if a curse would work on a demon but didn't think it would hurt to try. I'm also the one who left you the cards. They were meant to act as a warning. I didn't trust Whitby from the start and figured Dru had to have something to do with him, other than wanting the wand. When I realized I wouldn't have time to leave each card for you as I'd planned, I took you for the reading." Tash was breathing heavily, his back moving into my chest with each gulp of air.

"So, you didn't find The Tower in the drawer. You had it in your pocket?"

He grunted a yes.

"But, how could you have known we would be working together?"

"I didn't know, exactly. After Grace was taken, I read my own cards. My interpretation was that someone else would be involved with the wand, someone not human, and someone good."

I wanted to believe Tash; I really did. I felt at a loss for what to do. This was without a doubt the strangest job I had ever worked. War was not only herself, but Dru and Whitby, as well. She did everything she could think of to guarantee herself a win; kidnapping Tash's daughter, then using both of us to extinguish the lives of the creatures she saw as a threat to her new kingdom. I shook my head.

Ileana was sitting up with Tindrah's help. She looked over at me, her palm pressed against the side of her head. "I think he's telling the truth, Selene. War wanted to kill me as soon as they got me here, but Tash convinced her I would be worth more alive if you were to come around causing more problems. He was gentle with me, too. War was the one who smacked my head into the ground."

Tash bowed his head, still in my grasp. "I just want Grace back. You can have the wand, and anything else I can give. I need my daughter."

I felt the heartbreak in his words and released him. Tash took a couple of steps away from me and massaged his arms. I kept my body rigid, ready to fight off an attack. But none came.

"War still thinks I'm on her side." He looked down at his spilled herbs. "I was putting together another binding spell until you scattered it. I don't have any more stunning powder, but I think I can bind her fast enough."

"How quickly can you mix another?" I asked.

"Very."

"Do it, now."

Tash crouched down in a new location, drawing his pentacle in the dirt and pinching fresh herbs into his mortar.

I looked at Ileana, who groaned. "We will have to retie you. Tindrah and I will hide until War is in sight. Tindrah, you take the girl and fly her away while I get War inside the circle. Will that work, Tash?"

Our eyes met, and I felt a warmth in my heart. "Thank you, Selene. After you have Ileana taken care of, come over here and help me with the salt circle. It doesn't have to be visible. We can bury it in the dirt, so War won't know it's there."

Tindrah and I went to work. Ileana lay back on the stone slab. Tindrah put the gag back in place while I retied her hands. Then we went to Tash. Taking a rock, I drew a circle into the dirt around him, carefully remaining outside. Tindrah walked behind me, filling in my little ditch with salt. On my second pass, I scooped the dirt back over the salt, obscuring it from view.

When I finished, Tash and I looked into each other's eyes. Neither of us spoke. I nodded, turning on my boot heel to join Tindrah behind the tree line. I took my place behind a giant tree trunk as Tindrah flew up to perch on a limb, holding some boughs in front of her gray and white feathers. From there, she would have a straight shot down into the clearing. She and I would move as one, taking War by surprise. Or so we hoped.

A.D. BRAZEAU

CHAPTER SEVENTEEN

The sounds of a struggle came from the forest below. Grunting, whimpering, and War gnashing her teeth. Grace was not an easy victim, it seemed.

War walked into the clearing, the little girl flailing under her arm. As I watched, the little girl got in one good kick to War's lower back, her hair swinging with her effort. The demon looked down at her prey with a snarl, and I feared Grace wouldn't make it much farther.

Tash was on his feet the instant he saw his daughter. "Grace!" He started to move toward her, then checked himself.

Grace twisted her head in the direction of her father's voice. "Daddy!"

Before War could speak or move, Tindrah and I were off. Tindrah moved faster than I thought she could, swooping down from the tree and diving at War and the girl. War whirled to face her, not easing her grip on Grace.

As this was happening, I was running full stop at War. She shifted her attention to me and stepped back, as she was thrown off by what to do. In doing so, she loosened her grip on Grace and Tindrah was able to snatch the child out of her arms. The look on War's face one of shock.

With Grace out of harm's way, I barreled into War, shoving her into the salt circle. She fell with a thud onto her back but wasn't stunned for long. Although she was trapped inside, she wasn't immobilized like she was last time. Tash had to work fast.

Tash cut into the flesh of his palm, collecting the blood in his mortar, which he mixed with his herbs. War was on her feet.

As she sprang toward Tash like a panther, he flung the contents of the mortar in the air and began to recite the words of his spell. With War only an inch from strangling him, a mystical rope materialized and coiled itself around War's body, trapping her arms by her side. She thrashed her head back and forth and kicked her legs to free herself.

Eventually, she stopped trying to fight it and looked toward me. "You're making a mistake, Selene. I can offer you so much. You could join me and my sisters as an equal. Think of all we could do."

"No thanks. You can't even free yourself from a witch's spell. I think I'll pass. Is there anything you can do to silence her tongue?" I asked Tash.

He reached into his bag of tricks and pulled out a roll of mundane silver tape. "Actually, there is. Now that the spell is worked, you can step inside the circle."

I reached inside War's latex cloak, wrapping my hand around the Necromancy Wand. "Got it."

With War's mouth closed and her body and powers bound, I freed Ileana, once again. "The spell will hold for as long as I will, so we have a good amount of time, but not forever," Tash reminded me.

Bran castle was close. Carrying War over my shoulder, we should be there in about twenty minutes.

Tash looked wary. "I need to go with you, but I'm afraid to leave Grace."

Ileana reached out her hand, grasping Tash's shoulder. "If you'll trust me, Tash, she'll be safe. Grace and I will return to Selene's place and wait for you. The danger has passed."

Tash nodded and at that moment, small feet could be heard running through the dirt. "Dad!" Grace came running out of the forest, her pink tennis shoes leaving tracks in the dirt. It had been a long time since I'd been around children but thought she must be around seven or eight.

Tash spun around and scooped his daughter into a tight embrace. Grace's little face scrunched up into his neck and shoulder, her eyes shut tight.

Ileana and I moved away, allowing them this moment. Tindrah followed not far behind the child and joined us. "Do you need anything more from me, strigoi?"

"Tindrah, you can call me Selene. I do need one more thing. Tash will need a way to get swiftly to the castle."

Tindrah closed her eyes and inclined her head.

"All right, let's get on with this," Tash said, releasing his daughter to stand next to him. "Grace, this is Ileana and Selene. Ileana is going to take you to a house, where I will meet you in a little while. Selene and I have to send War back to where she came from."

The little girl's eyes slid toward War, bound and gagged in the dirt. "Good," she said.

Ileana held out her hand, and with a little prodding from her father, joined Ileana to walk back to the city. They had nothing more to fear in these woods.

I took up War, slinging her over my shoulder, and was off. Tindrah, Tash clasped in her great talons, flew overhead.

The castle was everything I imagined it to be. The gothic stone fortress was immense with the same red roofing of every building in Brasov. The structure was built on a cliff with round towers and an observation post. I couldn't wait to get inside.

Tindrah released Tash in the front courtyard, where I waited with War still over my shoulder.

"I'll wait for you here," said Tindrah, closing her wings

around her body next to a bush.

I could hear War gnashing her teeth underneath the tape, but that wasn't going to get her anywhere. I forced the giant wooden doors and we entered Dracula's castle.

The foyer was out of a movie. Dark, heavy furniture blended in with the dark wood floors. There were huge iron chandeliers outfitted with modern electricity. A musty smell of earth and wet stone permeated the surroundings. I would have loved to explore, but we had a mission.

Tash led the way, using the flashlight from his phone to find the entrance to the dungeons. We made our way down curving stone staircases until we reached our destination.

"This is definitely it," Tash said over his shoulder.

I could feel it, too. There was magic here. The space pulsed with it, sparking before our very eyes. Tash pulled the wand from his back pocket and began to swirl it in the air, electricity crackling like fire in front of him. He recited more of his magical words.

A portal opened. It looked like a black hole, rimmed by flames. This portal did not have the same lovely effect of the veil. Instead, it appeared every bit what it was, an entrance to Hell. Not wasting any time, I took War and flung her through the blackness. She disappeared, out of our sight in a demon realm.

"How do we seal it?" Tash asked, still grasping the wand.

I held my hand out. "I have an idea."

Tash looked at the wand, then back at me. "We could use this for so much."

"I know, but what we need right now is more important."

Tash looked back at the wand, and for a moment, I was worried. "You're right," he said before flinging the wand into the hole. With a bright flash of light, the portal closed in on itself.

Tash reached for my hand in the darkness. I could see him, but I knew he was blind as a bat down here.

"I hope you can forgive me, Selene. I didn't want to

betray your trust. I had to keep Grace a secret for fear of what might happen to her."

I squeezed his hand, pulling him in a little closer. "There's nothing to apologize for. I would have done the same in your shoes." I put a hand to Tash's cheek and leaned in to kiss him.

My intention was only a sweet peck on the lips. Instead, he slid his arms around my waist, crushing me firmly against his body. I weakened, allowing myself to open up in a way I never had before. His lips were full and hungry as he parted my lips, moving his tongue over mine. I melted into him. When I was afraid I would no longer be able to control myself, I broke the kiss, taking a step back.

Tash chuckled. "I get it. This isn't the place for a romantic interlude, although neither was the woods. Ever been to Baton Rouge?"

"Is that an invitation?"

"Yes, ma'am, it is." Tash brought my hand to his lips, sending a chill of pleasure down my spine.

How I longed for normalcy. A normal life, it seemed, was not for me. "Unfortunately, I'll have to take a raincheck. My brother's progeny has gone missing in France. I'm going to meet Alexandre there now. They're already waiting for me."

"Would you like some help? I've heard witches can be pretty useful, sometimes. Grace will love a trip to France."

My heart was full to bursting. I threw my arms around Tash's neck. "You would really come with me to help a bunch of vampires?"

Tash's face was turned into my neck. His breath was hot, sensual. "You bet your life I would."

We said our goodbyes to Tindrah. She was happy to return to her flock in the mountains of Romania, with a new sense of freedom. Before taking her leave, she bowed before me as one would a queen.

"Thank you, Selene. You have saved our kind. If you

ever find yourself in need of a friend, I will be here."
Tindrah took to the sky and was gone.

It was harder to say goodbye to Ileana. Tash and I found her and Grace curled up on the little couch in the living room of my cabin, watching videos on Ileana's phone.

Grace ran back into her father's arms while Ileana joined me in the bedroom. I pulled out my trunks, ready to pack them full of my precious volumes. There would be no rest, no basking in the glow of our victory.

"Ileana, I want you to do something for me." I turned toward her, grasping her hands in mine. "I want you to go to school. I would like to offer you a scholarship."

"You mean charity," she said, a wry look on her face. She squeezed my hand, then released it so I could continue packing. "I appreciate your generosity, Selene. But I can do it on my own."

"Of course, you can. At least allow me to pay you for your work on this case. I always pay my assistants, and very well. The rest, we can call a loan, if you like. You shouldn't waste any more time. Get out there and live your dreams."

She turned back to me, warmth spread across her face. "A loan, which I will pay back. That I can accept."

I enveloped her in a hug, her hair fragrant against my cheek.

CHAPTER EIGHTEEN

With War out of the way, Tash, Grace and I were able to meet the others in France. A relaxing trip to Baton Rouge would have to wait. There was a new problem. What had happened to Alexandre's former love?

After Annie, Thayer, and Jack went to Alexandre in Wexford, the four of them, with Bria in tow, went back to the chateau outside Annecy.

Upon waking, I would use my preternatural gifts to get myself to the immortals in the span of an hour. Tash and Grace would have a head start by train and would meet me there. If all went according to schedule, we should arrive at nearly the same time.

After Ileana left the cabin, Tash and I talked quietly in the bedroom while Grace slept on the couch. The sun would be rising soon. Tash would be taking my trunks with him on the train. This was a giant step for me in the trust category.

"I appreciate your help, Tash. I'm sure you're ready to get home to your family and coven." I sat next to Tash on the small bed.

He smiled a half-grin. "Not exactly. My coven doesn't know I'm here. I left to secure a magical object and give it to a demon without their consent. You can imagine how not thrilled they are."

I plucked at the hem of a legging. "They're probably mad as hell. But I'm sure all will be forgiven once you fully explain."

Tash put his arm around me, drawing me closer to the side of his body. "I'm sure they'll get over it pretty quickly. Then, I get to explain this." He squeezed my waist and I laughed.

"They'll get over this, too. It's a new age in more ways than one. If I don't lose it, all will be well."

Tash narrowed his eyes, leaning back a fraction of an inch. "What do you mean?"

"Just something that's been on my mind a lot lately. I've reached that age where others I've known have gone mad. Time weighs on the mind."

Tash leaned forward to kiss me. Before his lips met mine, he hesitated. "I've heard this before. I want to help you, Selene. In more ways than one. I think, given enough time, I can come up with a spell for you." He pressed his warm mouth to mine. I felt like I was home for the first time in my very long life.

After Tash and Grace left for the train station, I slept. The next night, I was up running and jumping with such speed, there was no time to take in the surrounding landscape. This was par for the course. My life generally found me rushing from one location to the next without time for more touristy pursuits.

I didn't know Millicent personally. What I did know of her came from Alexandre's brief descriptions. Although no longer in love with her, he would always care for her deeply. She was an important part of his life.

If his texts were any indication, he was worried beyond reason over her welfare. This alone compelled me forward. If she meant so much to him, she must be good people.

I didn't let up until I was standing on the circular drive

in front of the charming chateau. Tulips were beginning to push their way up through the soil along the front of the house. These were interspersed with leafy, green bushes that I knew would be in flower soon. The home was charming, inviting, and typical French country.

A child's laughter echoed inside. Tash and Grace were already here. As I moved toward the door, it opened, revealing Alexandre backlit from the crystal chandelier hanging over his head in the foyer. He held out his hand, beckoning me forth.

"Thank you for coming, Selene." He pulled me into a fierce hug. My brother may be human now, but he was still powerfully built. "The others are in the kitchen."

The house was a work in progress. Off the foyer to the left, I peered into an empty room. There were tarps spread on the floor along with a couple of paint cans. A ladder rested against a peeling wall. To the right sat a large, beautiful living room with sumptuous, deeply cushioned furniture and blue-and white-striped wallpaper.

"This way." Alexandre led me down the re-finished hallway freshly painted a delicate robin's-egg-blue.

The kitchen was also newly renovated. Everything was light and bright. Pristine Carrera marble countertops shone. White cabinets and modern pendant light fixtures made the room look larger, more open. The Viking range caught my eye. I'd wanted to get one for the house in Wexford, but the top-of-the-line appliance was a bit out of my budget.

Alexandre spoke again. "Selene, this is Annie."

Annie sat on a stool at the bar top with Grace next to her. They were playing tic-tac-toe while Grace ate a peanut butter and jelly sandwich. Annie slid off the stool, reaching for my hand with her own. She was a lovely woman whose warmth shone through her eyes.

"Selene, what a pleasure to meet you," she said as we shook hands. This was the rebel spy who had vanquished Emilia Romanov. There were countless questions I wanted to ask her.

Before I could talk with her more, Alexandre was pulling me toward a huge man standing at attention behind Annie. I recognized a soldier when I saw one. This man had been Emilia's progeny, the one Annie had saved from over two hundred years of torment. His sleepy eyes met mine. "Thayer Emmerich," he said with a strong German accent.

I smiled as we grasped hands. I sensed he was a man of few words. Tash sat at a round pedestal table behind Thayer. With him was a man with reddish hair, who I assumed to be Jack. His face was drawn, his eyes red. He stared down at his hands.

I moved toward him, my hand outstretched. "Jack, I presume."

Jack rose to meet my hand with his own. Alexandre mumbled something like, "This is Jack Thomas." Jack's eyes slid toward Alexandre.

I realized how awkward this must be for them. I believed the last time they were in each other's presence, Jack removed Alexandre's head with an ax. I stepped back, taking them all in. Never had I been in a room with so many immortals. Throw in the witch and this was really bizarre.

"It's wonderful to meet all of you. I wish it were under different circumstances." I placed my hand on Tash's shoulder, which he covered with his own. We were only in the beginning of our relationship, but I already felt like I could lean on him.

Annie pulled Thayer toward the stool she was previously occupying. "Thayer, you sit here with Grace while the rest of us go out to the lake."

His eyes went wide as he looked at Annie. She shook her head. "You'll be fine. I'm sure Grace won't bite."

Laughter erupted from everyone except Thayer. Even Jack chuckled. Annie patted the stool next to Grace. "We'll be right back."

She then led the way out the French doors that opened to the back terrace. Alexandre and Jack went after her.

Tash stood, grasping my hand. On our way past Thayer,

who sat rigidly on the stool, Tash clapped him on the shoulder. "Anything happens to my daughter and I'll put a spell on you you'll never shake." Tash smiled wickedly.

I pulled him after me. "Witches," I heard Thayer say under his breath.

Another peal of laughter from Grace brought a smile to my lips.

The back of the chateau was a wonderland. The green lawn was perfectly clipped in juxtaposition to the wildness of the woods beyond the property line. The starlight reflected off the surface of the lake to a lovely effect. I could imagine the many moonlit walks the occupants had enjoyed here.

Annie and Jack stood next to each other at the lake side, Alexandre slightly removed. As Tash and I approached, Annie pointed to the spot between them. I wondered how Alexandre and Annie were feeling around each other.

"This is the exact place I last saw Mills. I was in my room, there." She indicated a window on the second floor. "The sun had just set. I yelled down that I would join her for a stroll. When I got here, minutes later, she was gone. I thought it odd she wouldn't wait for me. I searched all around the property. When I couldn't find her nor any trace of her, I panicked and went to Jack. He was on the phone with the contractor and hadn't seen her since they rose. We grabbed Thayer and the three of us searched the property again. Then we went into Annecy. Nothing. All three of us attempted to contact her telepathically. Again, nothing. I'll admit my first thought was Alexandre had done something to her."

"Mine, too," Jack interrupted, glaring at my brother.

Annie placed a hand on Jack's arm and continued. "Being that he's human now, I couldn't imagine how he could possibly hurt her. Out of ideas, we went to him, anyway. Our hope was he would have some idea of where she could be. He was as shocked as we were. And now, here we are. Still, no trace of her. Millicent was known for wandering off, back before Jack. She wouldn't do that now. She no longer has any reason to." Annie, so steady up until now, broke. Blood tears spilled down her face.

Jack, his gaze trained at the ground the whole time, hooked his arm around her tiny waist.

Tash spoke up. "There's a couple of spells I can try. The most obvious one to start with is a locator spell. It won't take long to set up. I'll go grab my bag. We'll want to do it right here." Tash jogged back toward the chateau.

"Convenient, Sis, dating a witch. Think of all the things we can use him for." Alexandre was still Alexandre, albeit his fire was a little dimmer. His worry over his progeny was written all over his face.

"Where's Bria?" I asked. "I thought she was coming."

Annie, trying her best to smile through her tears, said, "I put her to bed in one of the guestrooms. Poor thing was exhausted."

Tash came running across the lawn, his black duffle bag gripped in one hand. "Okay, here we go." He panted a little, trying to catch his breath as he dropped down to his knees. "Everyone take two big steps back. Annie, Jack, I almost forgot. I'll need something of hers. Hair is preferable, if vampires shed like the rest of us."

Jack nodded. "I'll grab her brush." He took a flying leap up to the second-story terrace.

Tash watched him go, shaking his head. "That's not weird or anything."

Alexandre laughed, looking toward me. "I like him."

While we waited for the brush, Tash opened his bag. He took out a map of the world, spreading it over the very spot Annie had pointed to. There was nothing special about the map. It appeared as any ordinary atlas you might purchase from a rack at a gas station.

Jack was back in a flash, a fine silver hairbrush clutched in one hand. Tash grabbed it from him, pulling two long golden hairs from the tines. These went into his mortar. Tash pulled out his athame, slicing through the pad of his index finger. I found it interesting how crucial blood was for both of us. Several drops of dark liquid fell into the bowl with a plop. He held his finger up for me to lick.

With his pestle, Tash ground this concoction together. He whispered a few words and steam began to rise from the recesses of the bowl. Tash raised the mortar, tipping it over to spill out one small drop. The strange brew oozed out onto the map.

Tash repeated the words. The bloody mixture began to slowly move around the world. I followed it with my gaze, knowing the others were equally as entranced. The blob came to rest inside France. In unison, we all bent down for a closer look.

"Burgundy," said Alexandre. "That's where she's from. Did anyone check out the area of the old chateau? Or the cabin, maybe?"

Jack nodded his head. "We went there before going to Ireland. There's nothing but fields now. The cabin was empty."

"Well, we may have to go back," I offered. "She may not have been there when you looked, but she's certainly there now." I stopped, jolting upright.

"What, Selene?" Alexandre's voice was sharp, scared.

"I'm not sure. Maybe nothing. We need to check this first to rule it out."

Annie stepped forward. "I'll go. It isn't far. Don't go anywhere." She sped off into the night.

Alexandre moved forward, the tips of his boots touching the edge of the map. I gazed down, gnawing at my lip.

"Selene, tell me what you're thinking."

"Let's wait for Annie. She'll be back soon." I turned around, unable to look at Alexandre or Jack. *Please let Annie find her*, I thought.

The fifteen minutes we stood by the lake waiting for Annie felt like an eternity. Soon though, grass crunched under feet, and plants and tree limbs swished as she rushed back into view.

"Nothing. I looked around the whole area, cabin included."

I squeezed my eyes shut, bowing my head. "I think she's exactly where the spell says she is. Only not when."

"What do you mean, not when?" A look of dread crossed Jack's face.

"Nephthys," Tash offered.

"The goddess of death?" Alexandre blurted.

I sighed. This was all my fault. "Yes. We called her forth in Romania to help with the situation there. She was none too pleased. To teach me a lesson, she pulled me back in time. Before I was changed, to Ancient Rome. Tash brought me back. So, he can do it again. Right, Tash?"

He blinked at me with a wrinkled forehead. "I can try. It took a lot out of me, Selene. I think it also helped that you called her to you in Rome. While there, she was distracted enough for my spell to work. We will certainly make the attempt, but we have to be prepared for a different outcome."

"We can't leave her there," Jack breathed.

"I'll do my best." Tash looked up at him, still sitting on his knees in the grass.

Thayer and Grace had exited the chateau and were making their way toward us.

"You guys, I feel weird," Annie said, her voice shaky.

Alexandre reached for her. As he did so, his hand went right through her, as if she were an apparition. Her mouth was opened in a scream, then she was gone.

Thayer rushed forward. "What happened? Where did she go?" He frantically looked all around.

"Oh my God," Jack groaned. "Will she pull us all back in time?"

"Not if I can help it." Tash pushed the map aside and pulled a cloth from his bag. He wiped out the mortar, took up his blade and sliced into the palm of his hand. Blood flowed freely into the bowl. Tash dipped a finger into the blood and drew a symbol onto the grass as he recited another incantation.

The air around the six of us sparked and flashed. My skin felt electrified. I tingled from my toes upward.

"Ouch," Grace said, brushing some invisible force from her arms.

When the tingle reached the top of my head, it died away.

"We're all bound to this realm and time. She can't pull anyone else back." Tash slumped over, his breathing heavy.

I sank down next to him, pulling his head into my lap. "Are you all right?"

He nodded. "I am. It may take some time, and more help, but we'll get them back. There's no way I'll let Nephthys win."

"No, we won't." I held on to Tash, looking at the others. *Hold on, girls, we're coming.*

A.D. BRAZEAU

EPILOGUE

The nights were filled with a quiet anxiety. Tash left to secure some help. He was sure he could convince one or two of his witchy brethren to assist us in bringing back Annie and Millicent. The spell was difficult and the more hands he had, the better.

Poor Grace had adapted her schedule and spent most of the day sleeping so she could be awake with her "dark friends", as she called us vampires. She remained mostly aloof but still wanted to be near us. Grace seemed fine with being left behind, trusting her father and his judgment implicitly. I don't think I would have been quite so unsuspicious at her age.

Bria slept most of the day and night as she continued to be uncomfortable in her early pregnancy. Alexandre spent most of his nights with me. I suspected he was unable to sleep and worried he would wear himself down.

The evening Tash left for the airport, Alexandre and I sat in the living room. He lay stretched out on the sofa, while I sat cross-legged on the floor. I looked up at my brother as he stared at the ceiling. "You know we're going to get them back, Alexandre. It's only a matter of time."

He nodded, not making eye contact, his hands clasped

over his chest. "I do. We must believe that if Tash did it once, he can do it again. I'm just nervous. Annie will be fine, I've no doubt. She knows what's going on. But Mills. We must assume she doesn't have a clue what happened to her. Add her old life to the shock of being pulled back in time." Alexandre shook his head. "Who knows what she's thinking."

"She's smart, right?"

"She is."

"Then she'll figure it out. I already know she's tough because she put up with you for so long."

Alexandre chuckled. "Good point. It's horrible feeling so helpless."

"We're not helpless. We're re-grouping. This group, working together? We'll get them back, easy peasy." It wasn't going to be easy, but I knew in my heart the answer would be found. The road may not be simple, but we would walk it.

Thayer and Jack stuck together, for the most part. I wanted to reassure them, too, but they were not yet my people. Maybe in time, they would be.

When I had enough of melancholy men, I retreated to my room with Grace. She would break out her markers, and I would write to pass the time. Tash would only be gone for a couple of days. Still, this seemed like a good opportunity to re-focus my thoughts and begin recording my history. It was time to go back, not to regurgitate the story as I had so many times, but to remember with my heart. I set aside an excerpt for Alexandre to read:

AD 8. Caesarea, Mauretania

I stood looking out at the sea, fever wracking my body. Sweat trickled down my face, my eyes blurry and my head on fire. I refused my servants, forcing them to leave me in peace. My time was near.

The breeze off the water felt like heaven. My limbs grew heavier by the moment until I was forced to sit on the marble floor, unable to stand any longer. The ground was cool, and it felt like heaven against my bare legs. I lay down and pressed my cheek to the stone. My fingers found the scarab ring, hanging from a gold chain around my neck. I was forced to hide all ties to my past, but this I could never part with. I pulled it up, my gaze focusing on the lapis, memories of childhood washing over me.

I heard the soft pad of bare feet behind me. It was not my wish that anyone should contract my illness. "I told you to leave. I won't have you all dying to care for me."

"I am no servant, daughter of Cleopatra."

Too weak to move, I remained as I was. Two small, dirty feet came to a rest in front of my face. "Who are you?" I whispered. I could feel the life leaving my body.

"I am Layla. I have come to give you eternal life and take you to your brother."

"My brother," I croaked out the words.

"Do you wish to come with me, my divine one?" Her voice was so small, so childish.

I could do nothing but moan and nod my head. The rest was blackness.

I lost track of the years with Layla. Her cave was a sort of prison, a prison she imposed on herself. The others and I, we were not bound to stay with her, but remain, we did. I began to leave with more and more frequency, the freedom I craved only found off the island.

After the first years of being fearful of what I was and what I could do, I was learning, growing. I wanted to be free, to help people. I found I had a gift for this. My purpose was discovered. I returned for the last time to tell Layla goodbye. It would be difficult, but I knew I could make her understand.

Instead of the usual scene of blood-drinkers lounging about, I walked into a nightmare of death and charred bodies. My maker had immolated herself and her remaining followers. There was nothing to be done for them.

I spent most of my life a prisoner or bound to one being or another. I was a prisoner of Octavian, given away in marriage, unable to choose for myself, and finally, bound to my maker. For the first time in my existence, I was truly free of all constraints. I set out to live my own life, on my own terms. My name meant moon, and like the moon, I could not be contained.

BOOK ONE OF THE IMMORTAL KINDRED SERIES

True love never dies.

For Millicent, a once French noblewoman turned immortal vampire, forever is a long time to live in despair. The love of her life is murdered the night she becomes immortal. Millicent spends her endless night in a melancholy which never ends. Two hundred forty years later, she locks eyes with an English actor, who happens to look exactly like her long dead love.

Sadness turns to happiness as Millicent and Jack find passion in each other's arms. Their fling quickly turns serious as Millicent finds happiness once again—and possibly her one true love.

However, their relationship becomes complicated by her own uncertainty, Jack's mortality, and the other man in Millicent's life, Alexandre, her maker and companion. When Alexandre puts his foot down, Millicent must decide if she's going to continue to be led by others or take the reins and drive the outcome of her life.

Deepest Midnight is set in modern day Savannah, Ga with occasional glimpses back to 18th century France. This is the first book in The Immortal Kindred Series.

Available at all major book retailers

BOOK TWO OF THE IMMORTAL KINDRED SERIES

Always and Forever

Annie is a Culper Spy captured by Hessian soldiers. Powerful and mysterious Captain Thayer Emmerich takes mercy and releases her. Annie is inexplicably drawn to the handsome German, but she hates the feeling of powerlessness the enemy has left her with. Annie would give anything to be stronger.

One evening at the famous Green Dragon Tavern, Annie befriends the ethereal Millicent. Soon after meeting Millicent, Annie discovers her secret--her new friend isn't human. Millicent introduces Annie to her maker, Alexandre, and Annie joins their preternatural family.

Annie finally has the strength and freedom she

needs to aid the revolution and see Thayer, once again. The two discover a passion neither has known before. But, too many complications exist for the pair to find happily ever after. Not only are they fighting on opposite sides of the war, the evil Emilia Romanov has plans for Thayer that do not include a love affair.

Rebel Heart is set in 18th century Boston and Savannah, as well as modern day Germany and France. This is the second book in The Immortal Kindred Series.

Available at all major book retailers

BOOK THREE OF THE IMMORTAL KINDRED SERIES

Love has no limits...

Alexandre has retreated from the world. He has no one to love, nowhere to call home. While licking his wounds in the middle of nowhere, Alexandre is approached by Irish lass, Bria. She has a proposal for him; to follow her to Ireland and fight demons.

Alexandre finds this amusing, but intriguing. More than anything, he is curious to see the individual who sent Bria, someone from his ancient past.

In Ireland, Alexandre confronts a dilemma greater than fighting demons. He must face down fiends of all kinds, deciding once and for all who he really is. Sparks fly between Bria and Alexandre, adding to the already complicated situation. Can a bad boy vampire really change?

The King of Kings is set in southern Ireland with a glimpse back to Ancient Egypt.

Available at all major book retailers

ABOUT THE AUTHOR

A.D. Brazeau is an award-winning author who writes what she loves. From dark and fantastical fairytale retellings to quirky romance, and everything in between, she loves nothing more than to immerse herself in new worlds. A.D. Brazeau is a book-obsessed wife, mother, and dog lover, who grew up surrounded by stories. Not much has changed. A.D. is from Colorado Springs, Co, and currently resides in Orange County, Ca.